Xavier

Kadance Royal

ROYAL MEDIA
AND PUBLISHING LLC

Royal Media and Publishing
P. O. BOX 4321
Jefferson, IN 47131
502-552-1643
www.royalmediaandpublishing.com
royalmediapublishing@gmail.com

Cover Design: Elite Book Covers

ISBN: 978-1-955501-03-3

Printed in the United States of America

Dedication

I dedicate this book to every Man who wants, needs, actively looking and desperately wants to be loved and give love. ....

Acknowledgements

First, I acknowledge my Lord and Savior Jesus Christ for giving me all of my gifts and especially my gift to write His words.

My husband who is always supportive, loving and encouraging me to utilize all of my gifts and talents. Thank you honey.

To my mother, Dr. Daisy Foree, who is my number one cheerleader and always tells me, "hang in there, you can do it." To my father, Dr. Jack Foree, who is never far away from me in my spirit or heart. I only have to look in the mirror each day to see him.

To Rev. Claude and Mrs. Lillie Royston who support me in everything I do. To the rest of my family, I love you and thank you for your prayers, support and love.

Julia Royston/Kadance Royal

P. S. Why do I write with a pen name? It's about branding and keeping the brands separate. It's another way to create. God created me with many gifts, creative outlets and opportunities and I intend to use them all! Let's go!

Table of Contents

Introduction

Xavier is handsome, quiet, intelligent and lonely. He hides so much of himself to blend in, get by and survive. His life should have been so different but he has played with the cards that he has been dealt.

Scratching, clawing, working, striving, hiding, creeping, learning and yearning to be something more, have something more and be a whole person is his highest goal in the life. Accomplishing much with no love is not really living and thriving but just existing. Expectations, hopes and dreams have been dashed so many times with Xavier standing in the distance with empty hands gives him little chance of really hoping again.

Normalinda has worked, sacrificed, loved, waited and it looks like she finally will have another chance but at what risk and price.

Meet Xavier Hernandez in Book 3 of the Men of Roberts Junction Series. Enjoy!

Chapter 1

The Club

Xavier found himself in clubs more and more. Leaving Southern Indiana hadn't been his choice but a necessity. Seeing the second love of his life, Annette, with someone else was more than he could stomach. As a technology guru, he could easily find a job anywhere. So, he packed up a year ago and moved just a hundred miles north, to Cincinnati, Ohio.

Thursday night at the "V Club" was jumping. The darkness, loud music, people intoxicated and looking each other up and down hoping to catch somebody's eye was routine. Deep down they were all looking for something or someone to take home for the night or quite possibly for a lifetime but the night would do. He knew that he should take the last swallow from the glass, go home and handle the itch himself, but a tall but petite-framed brown face with a round behind and cantaloupe breasts caught his attention. She dropped her phone off the table and bent down to pick it up. Her low-cut top revealed even more of her breasts than the black tank top was hinting from under the leather jacket she wore in spite of the warm weather. Her tight jeans were making Xavier's jeans tighter and the bulge in his pants even bigger than before.

He thought, 'Oh yes.'

When she stood up, their eyes locked and a slight smile came across both their faces. She sat back down to continue to watch the others dance. He told himself it was wrong, but to be skin on skin with a soft female like that would suit him nicely. He didn't use the head that was on his shoulders, but he let the one below the belt do the ruling tonight. He put the glass on the bar after drinking the last bit and got the courage to walk over to the table.

He approached her from the left and bent slightly near her ear so that she could hear him. "Hello."

"Hey." The young lady looked up and smiled.

"What's your name and why are you here alone?"

"I like the music and I'm not alone. My friend is on the dance floor." She pointed to another beautiful brown young sister on the dance floor with a tall white dude that, in spite of the stereotype, could actually dance his butt off.

"Oh, I like the music too, and I like what you look like even more. What's your name?"

"Normally, I just go by Linda."

"Normalinda?" He must have been delirious, and he almost fainted because the only piece of his brain that was focused thought she'd said Normalinda.

"No, just Linda," she replied just enough to be heard above the loud music.

Xavier's heart became regular and his breathing returned to normal.

"What's your name?"

"Xavier."

"Oh wow, X marks the spot."

"Something like that. Would you like to dance?"

"Sure."

Xavier stood and extended his hand. Linda didn't take it but followed its direction to the dance floor, as she put her small crossbody bag with an extra-long handle across her right shoulder. The music changed to Eric Benet's soft, sexy voice that always set the mood so right for sex—sweaty and hot to be exact. He realized that his whole body was suddenly on alert even before he embraced her. She fit perfectly in his arms, and with her heels, her head landed a few inches above his chin. Xavier thought, *thank you, DJ, for a slow, soft song so I can just hold her and grind up on her and take the edge off this hard on.* He hated trying to dance to some fast song. He might be Mexican, but slow dancing was more his style.

He bent down a little to ask her, "You got a man?"

"No, not right now. Why? You got a woman?"

"I'm holding one right now who is beautiful as hell." In spite of the funky smells in the room, she smelled wonderful too. Linda giggled.

As he continued shuffling his feet as well as moving her around to the beat, Linda pushed her body closer to his. He didn't know if this was a signal or not, but he was taking advantage of it. He drew her in closer still and his hands landed somewhere near her waist, and hers ended up on his back perfectly. That was his cue and his penis came alive immediately. In the mood he was in, a woman could just walk by and get him hard. He remembered that he had condoms in his wallet, his car's glove compartment, and his house. Xavier tried to adjust himself, but Linda shifted her pelvis up against his crotch one too many times.

"Xavier, am I exciting you?"

"Too much."

Linda's friend walked over to her and tapped her on the shoulder. "Girl, you ready?"

"Uh no."

"I am, and you know the rule."

"What rule?" Xavier asked.

"We come together, we go home together," Linda said.

"I hate to hear that, but safety first. Can I have your number?"

"Sure." Linda pulled out a small card with her name and number on it and leaned in real close to whisper in his ear, "Call me any time because I want to see as well as feel what was in your pants."

"I will. You can guarantee it." Xavier watched her walk away and knew that it would be hand job time for him tonight instead of this beauty. He paid his tab at the bar and headed the short ten minute ride home.

Two hours later, the front doorbell of his condo rang loudly. Xavier looked at his phone to see that it was 4:00 a.m. *What the hell*, was his first thought. He pushed the button on the security alarm screen and there was a familiar face, but it was yelling, "Come on, bro! Let me in; it's the pizza man!"

Xavier knew that voice, face and the signal. Releasing the button as soon as possible, he grabbed his backpack keys and did only what he knew to do and that was to run. He heard one gunshot but kept running to his bedroom.

Opening the door of his closet, slid down the pole to the lower level of his condo. At the bottom of the pole, there was another slide that led directly to a door in Old Lady Russell's basement. Old Lady Russell was wheelchair bound on the first floor. She refused to move so her family made everything convenient for her on the same floor. No hinderances because it was a perfect escape route for him.

He didn't know when but God decided today would be the day that he would need this tunnel. *Shit,* he thought, *I just got new shoes and jeans.* Why should that matter now? There is nothing like fear to make you no longer care as you are breaking in a new pair of pants and shoes.

Breathing hard, he kicked open the cellar door to get to his garage and heard the sound that no one ever wants to hear. "Freeze!" Simultaneously, he heard multiple guns cocked and ready to fire.

"Shit!" was the last word he said.

"Put your hands behind your back. You are under arrest. You have the right to remain silent," the officer continued and Xavier closed his ears to the rest of the Miranda rights but opened his brain to get his thoughts together about what was next.

They arrived at the Cincinnati Police Station and went through the check in procedure for a new inmate. It had been nearly twenty years since Xavier had been in jail for any reason. The last time had been for public intoxication and disorderly conduct, but he knew that the charges would be far from that. His entire life had now come crashing in on him. There was nowhere to run or to hide. The years of lies, trauma, deceit and loss had now come to culminate and crescendo in this moment right here. But what was next? How did it get so out of control? What was real, and what was false?

When the doors of the cell closed, he asked one question of the guard, "I get a call, right?"

"Yes, but not for an hour. We'll come get you when you can make your call."

Chapter 2

Busted

With nothing but time on his hands, Xavier lay down on the hard board for a cot and closed his eyes. It was risky to close his eyes, but he took the chance because at least he was alone with his thoughts and memories. The cot was hard, stiff and cold but somehow his body relaxed. Why? He got caught. This was the end of the road. The day and time of reckoning. The piper was going to get paid one way or the other. He was alone but in a distance, he could hear the soft faint whisper of his mother calling him, "Xavier, my love. Where are you?" There was always no answer to her initial call because that was the game they often played when he was small. He smiled slightly to himself just hearing that sweet sound of his mother's voice even if it was in the distant past and coming only when sleep was near.

His mother's voice again, "My heart has a hole in it that only you can fill. Where is my Xavier?"

Still dreaming, Xavier smiled again ever so slightly to himself and could hear himself say out loud, "X marks the spot in my mother's heart." He wiped a small tear that suddenly formed in his left eye. He would have lied if accused of crying at this adult stage of his life, but right now, it didn't matter. There was no one around and, in fact, he no longer cared. He would have given anything to be in his mama's arms. So he settled for his mind taking him there where his body could never go again.

He saw his mother standing with her hands shaped like a heart on top of the left side of her faded white shirt where her beating heart was located. A smile on her face that could literally light up a room and definitely every cell in Xavier's being.

Back then, he always jumped out from under the bed or from behind an open door to his mother's laughter. She would be picking him up, hugging him so tight and kissing him on the cheek. Ironically, even in this jail cell, the sweet smell of lavender quickly came across his nose. It only lasted a second and then the smell of sterile metal and a faint odor of a previous resident replaced it which brought Xavier back to reality and his thoughts, *I'm caught.*

Forty years before, Xavier's mother Marquita was a young girl in Mexico. Her parents were not wealthy but handy and industrious. Her mother was Martina and her dad's name was Pablo.

Pablo was a miracle worker with anything with an engine. He could fix any type of equipment. With this skill, Pablo was a rich man. He found himself in places that were unbelievable to those in his small village. Pablo was the mechanic but

Martina knew what to do with her body. Pablo knew too well that Martina wasn't faithful, but she was loyal to him. Her escapades were known throughout the village because her mother had taught her well and her mother taught her mother before. With their skills, they could get any man they wanted. Martina only wanted Pablo, but she also wanted money, more money than Pablo could make.

When they married, they agreed that they would always be together, keep their money in the house, but how they made the money was their own story. Martina and Pablo had one beautiful daughter Marquita and two sons, Pedro and Miguel.

The rich loved to play in Mexico. Rich people don't live in Mexico, just come to have fun, eat well and be pampered while in Mexico. The Miller family was no different. They were wealthy horse people from Lexington, Kentucky who would come down to Mexico in the winter to play. Thomas Jefferson Miller had been coming to Mexico with his father for years. It was now his son Brandon Miller's turn to come and play in Mexico. They had a private house, maid service, cooks, grounds keepers and Pablo, who managed everything at the Miller Estate. The money was wonderful and Pablo made sure that everything was ready to satisfy all of the Miller's needs and wants while in Mexico.

"Pablo."

"Si, Senor."

"My boys are on their way down there. Andre and Antonio are coming along with them. Don't let nothing happen to them. I know that your daughter is gorgeous right now but try to keep Brandon away from her."

"I will try, Senor."

"Do your damndest."

"Si." Pablo hung up the phone and began yelling orders that the Americans were on their way.

After Mr. Jefferson Miller hung up, he tried to make the boys understand. "Brandon, don't let me have to come down to Mexico to get you or

Brandon and your other friend's dick out of any trouble, you hear me?"

"Yes, sir." Brandon winked at his friends over his father's head as he was getting boxes out of his desk drawer and wondered, *where did all of those condoms come from?* He shook his head quickly to remove the thought just like a fly off the back of one of the Thoroughbreds outside.

"I'm giving you the plane for safety and Antonio is going with you guys to interpret. If by some chance, God forbid, you have to get out in a hurry, Antonio will be there to help you. Those Mexican girls are as fertile as the girls in the Lexington projects. Use a condom every time. Did you hear me, every time? By the way, here is a box of condoms for each of you 'cause your dick don't know better. Neither of the three of you think with the head that's on top of your shoulders. Let me think for you."

Brandon snickered along with his two friends, Skip and Jason.

"You guys think it's funny? Let me have to send somebody to get you all from down there and it won't be funny. Believe you me, it will be the last paid trip you three go on. Hear me?"

"Yes, sir," the three answered in unison.

Brandon Miller smiled at his two friends and mouthed, 'yes' raising his fist in the air quickly when his father, Thomas Jefferson Miller, turned his back to get the cash out of his safe and to pitch them their individual box of condoms.

Of course, Brandon forgot about the mirror over the credenza. "Brandon, I saw that."

"Sorry, Dad."

"Your bags packed?"

"Yes, sir."

"You are only getting this trip because you brought your grades up out of the toilet this semester. I've got big plans for you and this business. Don't screw it up. Got it?"

"Got it."

Miller Sr. had a feeling in his gut that he was going to regret this trip, but he promised and when he made a promise, he kept it. Good or bad, his father taught him that *a man is only as good as his word*. He hoped that his son would finally learn that one day.

Brandon and his friends ran out the front door to the awaiting car. They didn't touch their bags because that's what the servants were for. These boys were a member of the social privileged. They knew how to ignore, look down on others or determine who was important and who was not. As Andre and Antonio looked on, they were hoping that they wouldn't need to help these boys too much or too many times this week. Andre and Antonio were the long-time eyes and ears in the States and in Mexico. They just looked at each other and shook their heads with no words needed as the boys talked all the way to the airport.

Andre and Antonio supervised the boarding of the luggage and before boarding, Andre turned to Antonio and said, "One of us has to say something. The boss sent them down here with us, but we've got our hands full."

"You are right, but will they listen?"

"No, but warn them at least."

"All right."

Brandon and his friends were driven by Andre. The boys talked all the way to the airport and aboard the private plane to Mexico, of all that they planned to do to the eager or not so eager young girls in Mexico. With a box full of condoms, they hoped it would last the whole week but who knows. Andre shook his head at their words and tried to get their attention as they came closer to landing.

"Boys, let me remind you are no longer in the United States. This is Mexico. I know that you are used to getting your own way and having your own way with the girls in Lexington, but this is not Lexington. The rules are different here than at home. Watch yourselves. Don't let any of them try to let you penetrate them without a condom. Hear?"

"Yeah, we hear you."

"But there is nothing like free styling without a condom. That pussy feels so good."

"Condom on every time, all of the time. Your dad will have my hide."

"I hear you."

"It is great without a condom, and that's the reason why I have three babies, but I am an old man with a wife. You guys have your whole lives ahead of you, hear?"

"We hear you, Popi."

"Okay, stay alert."

Meanwhile, at the Miller Villa...

"Marquita!"

"Yes, Ma!"

"The guests will arrive in an hour. The rooms are ready and your papa has gone to the landing strip to make sure everything is ready there, but have you swept the front porch?"

"No, not yet, Mama."

"Hurry!"

"Yes."

Marquita Hernandez found the broom in the closet and headed to the front porch and began sweeping as her mother instructed but stopped to use the bathroom on the way to the porch. *Another week of Americans to serve, pamper the women in spite of their rude behavior and avoid the men's advances*, Marquita thought.

The Hernandez family was fortunate that they had a plush place to work in the Miller Villa and not in the fields. Once finished in the bathroom, Marquita turned on the faucet to wash her hands. When she turned the spout to the right for the water to stop, it continued. "Oh no! Mama, help!"

"What happened?"

"The water spout is stuck again. I thought Pedro fixed it."

"Apparently not."

"This can't happen this week. Not right now. Run check the back field for Pedro and tell him to come quick."

Marquita ran out the back door of the house. When she arrived in the field, she found Pedro, her older brother, mowing the last bit of grass on the lawn. Waving to get his attention, she called, "Pedro! Pedro!"

Fortunately, Pedro saw her coming and turned off the tractor to hear, "What is the matter?"

"Come quick, the faucet won't turn off in the back bathroom! The guests will arrive in an hour!"

"Oh my goodness, Santa Maria. I thought that was fixed."

"It is not."

"On my way!" The tractor was turned off after he made a final row, and both of them ran towards the house. "Marquita, get my tool box in the closet."

"Will do." When the bathroom toilet and sink were fixed and the floor mopped, Marquita realized that she hadn't swept the front porch.

She ran to the front porch just as the cars pulled up in the driveway.

"Who is that?" Brandon asked with a smile.

"Marquita, my niece," Andre said hesitantly, but he knew that Brandon's eyes weren't playing tricks on him because she was beautiful. The best part about her was that she was sweet, down to earth, and didn't really realize how pretty and desirable she was. She could easily manipulate any man who gave her attention, but she spent her time helping her mother and father build a life.

"Oh my goodness, she is gorgeous," Brandon whispered to himself more than anyone else.

"Thank you, but she's off limits," Andre said as he walked away.

"Close your mouth, Brandon, you act like you've never seen a chick before," Jason said.

"That ain't no chick; that's a beautiful girl," Skip said.

"Shit, what I wouldn't do to have her under me," Brandon replied.

"You need to be grown ass men first before you can approach Andre's niece. Be careful,

Brandon. I've seen that look before," Antonio said.

"I won't hurt her, just please her," Brandon said.

"Really? In your dreams," Skip scoffed.

"Come, gentlemen, let's get settled," Antonio signaled.

The majority of the week, Brandon, Skip and Jason drank, partied and had sex with most of the girls in the village who would let them, except Marquita. It was Thursday, and Brandon's patience was wearing thin. He wasn't used to being turned down, not gotten anything that he wanted, or the worst, flat out ignored. Since they had arrived on Sunday, he noticed a pattern with Marquita. It was about time for her to clean the pool house.

"Stay here, fellows, I need some alone time."

"Be careful."

"I'm always careful. I got jimmies in my pocket and a tiger who is ready to roar."

"Well, I hope that she is ready and willing to accept what you have to offer."

"Irresistible, baby, I'm irresistible."

"We'll see."

Brandon followed Marquita into the pool house. She didn't see him right away because she was busy mopping the floor after having picked up all of the towels and trash left by the unruly occupants. She did hear the lock on the door pop.

"Hello, beautiful. How are you today?"

She turned to see the voice was that of the obnoxious Brandon Miller. She knew that he wanted her because he had let her know it all week, but this was his chance. She was vulnerable and he really felt entitled to her and everyone else in her village. She had heard about him in town and knew that it was just a manner of time. What would she do? Her family was at the Miller's mercy. She knew what her mother had always taught her. "Remember, Marquita. The woman always has the power." This time Marquita wasn't so sure.

"I'm fine. Can I help you?"

"Oh, yes, you can. We can make this hard or easy for both of us. Which is it going to be?"

"Easy. Let's go!" Marquita leaned the mop up against the wall, lifted her dress and her underwear fell to the floor.

"Oh my. I see that this is going to be like taking candy from a baby."

"Yeah, and I'm the sweetest candy you will ever taste."

"Come to Papa."

"Gladly. Take off your shirt, drop your pants and sit on the bench."

"Yes."

"Close your eyes."

When Brandon sat down, he was fully erect and all Marquita had to do was straddle him and ride him like a horse.

"You can get up now."

"No, I want you again." Marquita shifted her hips and tightened her pelvis just enough to squeeze his penis to erection.

"Hold on, aw shit, I'm already hard again."

"I knew it. You are a stallion baby just like your horses."

"I guess I am, and you'll be mine the rest of the week."

"Whatever you say." Marquita looked down and she could see that the condoms were still in his pocket. She rode him harder and faster this time and when they climaxed, she dug her nails into his back, creating an X.

"Shit, girl, you scratched me!"

"X marks the spot, baby."

"I got your spot, right here."

"That's what I'm talkin' about,"

That began round three and much more because they met every day in that pool house and those condoms never made it onto his penis, just on the floor. The sex was insatiable and Marquita had been taught well how to use what she had to get what she wanted. By the end of the week, Marquita knew every inch of Brandon Miller as well as what would make him scream, laugh and almost cry to be pleasured.

Marquita smiled to herself as she finally put her floral dress over her head while watching Brandon zip his shorts and almost stagger out of the door like a drunk man from their time together. "Damn, girl, you almost killed me that last time," Brandon said.

"I'm sorry, Popi," Marquita said sweetly, but secretly she knew that she was no longer the student but now the teacher.

Brandon opened the door, looked both ways, and immediately, was met with a large hand around his throat literally lifting him off the ground onto the pool house wall.

"What the?"

"What the hell is right. Didn't I warn you about these girls down here? Did you use a condom? I don't care how beautiful she is, you didn't protect yourself did you? Answer me!" Jefferson Miller screamed.

Marquita said nothing but began sweeping the floor violently. Andre and Antonio stood by saying nothing, but Andre knew that he would have to have a talk with his niece sooner rather than later.

"Dad, I didn't know you were here."

"Of course, you didn't. Your dick was otherwise occupied."

"When did you get here?"

"About an hour ago. I have a meeting tonight, and then we leave tomorrow. Understand?"

"Yes."

"Go to your room and pack your shit. Take a shower. You smell like pussy."

"Yes, sir." Brandon walked away with a sulk. He knew that his week of fun was officially over. No more freedom.

"Andre, whose girl is this?" Mr. Miller asked because Andre and Antonio were always nearby.

"My niece, sir," Andre said.

"You know what to do," Mr. Miller said as he lit his cigar and walked away.

"But, sir," Andre replied to Mr. Miller's back.

"But, sir, nothing. Handle it," Mr. Miller said, not looking back.

Andre and Antonio stood silently until Mr. Miller was well into the main house, then they quickly turned and entered the pool house.

"Marquita, what were you thinking?" Andre asked with a shout.

"He came on to me. What was I supposed to do, say no? It could have been worse," Marquita answered nonchalantly.

"Yes, I know, but did you at least use protection?" Andre continued with another question.

"No," Marquita said quietly.

"That is terrible! You could be pregnant right now and normally, girls who—"Andre continued to shout.

"Who do what, Uncle Andre? Who fuck with the boss' son get killed? Is that what you were getting ready to say?"

"Yes, that's what normally happens, but I can't do it. I just can't do it," Andre said.

"She has got to go somewhere, though, Andre. She can't stay here, and you've got to tell Pablo and Martina," Antonio insisted.

"You are right, Tonio, but where and who?" Andre said.

"I've got it. Grammy's old place, the ranch, in Laredo," Antonio said.

"The home for unwed mothers?" Marquita exclaimed.

"At least, you will live," Andre said sternly.

"No, I won't do it."

"You don't have a choice. If we don't take care of you, Mr. Miller will get someone else. I promise. His son is promised to a girl back in the States. You mean nothing. You were just a fling with his ding a ling."

"Thanks,"

"You are welcome, young lady, but you knew better and this time it is going to cost you."

"Cost me what."

"Your freedom, that's how much. Finish up in here and I'm headed to the house to break it to your parents,"

Andre and Antonio walked to the garage to find Pablo, who was cleaning and putting the final touches on the car for the evening's festivities.

"Pablo, we have a problem."

"What's the problem?"

"Marquita's been sleeping with Brandon Miller."

"What the hell!"

"Exactly."

"Boss will have her killed!"

"For sure. I suggest we take her to Grammy's ranch in Laredo."

"The place for unwed girls? Is she pregnant?"

"I don't know yet, but we can't wait around to see. He gave the order already."

"She must go now before tonight."

"Si."

"Martina!" Pablo took off running and yelling for his wife in the main house kitchen. Martina could hear Pablo long before she saw him.

"What, Pablo, what?" Martina replied just as loudly.

"Antonio says that Marquita has been screwing around with Brandon Miller. She has got to go to Laredo right away,"

"No other way?"

"Either that or death. Boss already gave the order."

"Get the car. I'll get her ready. Call the ranch."

They all moved around the house quietly but in a vast hurry and hopefully unbeknownst to Mr. Miller. Everyone in the house knew that getting Marquita to the ranch was a matter of life and death.

Meanwhile, because of the number of people in the house and the importance of the guests, Marquita was driven by her brother Pedro, instead of her parents, to the ranch.

"Pedro, you're not going to talk to me?"

"Nope."

"Why not?"

"Because you are my sister. I love you, but I don't have the words to say how mad, sad and scared I am for you right now."

"I appreciate your honesty, but I didn't mean to put myself in danger. I was just having fun enjoying myself."

"Not with that guy. Not with these kinds of people. They are killers! They care about no one but themselves. It was fun, but at what price, Marquita? You cost us a lot! First off, you. Second, you're probably pregnant, and finally, our jobs. You were not thinking at all! Andre was supposed to kill you, put a gun to your head and bury you without our knowing. They could kill him for not killing you. Now, do you understand?"

"Yes."

Pedro and Marquita said not another word the remainder of the trip. Once Pedro started going down the dirt road, the dust ball seemed to get bigger and wider, welcoming Marquita to the big house, farm, and Ms. Venezuela.

Marquita knew that she had gone too far with her time with Brandon. The orders were given, the decision was made, and she would be at the ranch for as long as it took. Pedro handed Ms. Venezuela a brown envelope and then he hugged Marquita tightly. Her bags were already at the bottom step of the house. He wiped his eyes on his sleeve and said only, "Goodbye."

Left alone, Marquita watched the truck drive back down the driveway just as fast, with more dust and gravel. With only her thoughts and to wonder what would happen next. she settled into her new life at the ranch.

At the main house, Brandon looked everywhere for Marquita. It was his last night in Mexico and he wanted just one more round, just one more taste and one last kiss.

It was late when he snuck out of the house to the servants' quarters to sneak inside Marquita's room. He knocked three times on the door just like other times, but there was no answer. He turned the knob of the door and it eased open like before. It was dark, but there wasn't much furniture and the bed was the largest object in the room. There was no warm greeting at the door like there had been the hot nights before, and he could tell that the bed was made from the dim light from the parking garage.

Suddenly, a light came on and a familiar voice said, "So, she hasn't been chasing you. You've been chasing her."

"No, Dad, it really wasn't like that."

"Oh, , son, I know what's it like, and I warned you before you came that you were not supposed to taste the forbidden fruit, but you didn't listen."

"Dad, she is so beautiful and fun."

"Yes, and fertile. I won't have a bastard grandchild here in this city or country."

"You won't."

"How did you know? Did you even use protection?"

"Once or twice, but she felt so good and made me come so fast."

"Oh hell, I can't listen to any more of it. I have to go into town for a late meeting, but she's gone."

"Where, Dad, where?"

"You don't have to worry about where because you'll never see her again."

"No, Dad, please!" Brandon grabbed his father just as he was about to walk out the door.

Brandon's father punched him in the mouth and he fell to the floor. "Have you lost your mind putting your hands on me? Get your ass up off the floor. I'm not some kid on the football field. I am your father and don't you ever forget it! We're already late to a meeting, so get up and open this door!"

Brandon wiped his mouth with his hand and saw the fresh red blood that had oozed from his wound. He still had all of his teeth, but they had been loosened by the punch. He had been warned and he knew better, but he couldn't help himself. He had wanted Marquita so badly for their last night that was never to be.

Pedro was right.

Each day, week and month, Marquita's belly grew and grew until one day, she told Ms. Venezuela, "It's time."

"I'll get everything ready."

Ten hours later, Marquita delivered an eight pound boy, light brown hair, brown eyes and an odd-shaped mark over his left shoulder. He cried like normal and screamed even louder when Ms. Venezuela slapped him on the bottom.

"His lungs are strong."

"Is that good?"

"That's great."

As Venezuela continued to cleaned the baby, she said, "He's marked."

"What does that mean?"

"It means that even though his father is not here, your baby has the family mark on him anyway."

"Is that bad?"

"Not necessarily. It just means that you'll have to be careful with him. You be sure and stay here because they may come for him."

"They don't want my baby."

"Their blood runs through his veins along with yours. You mean nothing to them, but a boy is an heir and that means everything in their world."

Marquita was quiet for a long time. As the baby grew, she didn't go anywhere except the market and then returned back to the ranch. She named the baby Xavier. He was in her heart and she always reminded him every day that, "X marked the spot." Marquita took her two fingers and made the X over her heart every day to Xavier to remind him of just how much he was truly loved. She was lonely, home sick and regretted ever meeting Brandon Miller. Any feelings of anger, disappointment or regret left immediately when she looked into her little Xavier's eyes. Pure love from a child to his mother.

Over the years at the ranch, there were few visitors, only two other young women who were also sent to the ranch to have their babies in private by very wealthy families who didn't trust any organization in the States to keep the baby, the woman and the situation a secret. They came to the ranch shortly after Marquita arrived. One was named Rachel, a black girl from Chicago, and the other was Laura, from old Southern money in Atlanta. They formed a sisterhood of sorts because of the situation surrounding their pregnancies. Ms. Venezuela kept the full details a secret and was paid extremely well to do so.

The girls didn't want to talk about the story surrounding their babies, their families and the rejection by the father of their child that they were carrying. Everyone kept to themselves until the babies were born.

It was an exciting time when the babies were born, but six weeks after the births, the babies and mothers left the ranch. Marquita stayed. Ms. Venezuela and the life at the ranch was peaceful, quiet, with strict rules but still not home.

Chapter 3

The Next Phase

Five years later...

Ms. Venezuela was getting older and moving slower. She was no longer taking young women onto the ranch no matter how much money the family was willing to pay. She told Marquita many times, "This ranch will be yours one day."

Marquita would smile but say nothing.

At five years old, Xavier was becoming a handful. Marquita was glad that she was young and slim, with much energy, because she could hardly keep up with Xavier. He loved to laugh, run and play. Hide and seek was his favorite game. When he was one or two, he would just hide under the sheets or under the clothing in the laundry basket. By the time he was five, he was hiding under the bed, in closets, or one time in the cupboard under the sink. Venezuela would sit in her rocking chair, watch him run, look at him and laugh, but Marquita would chase him down so she wouldn't lose him and he wouldn't hurt himself.

"Xavier, where are you?" Marquita said in that special voice that always seemed to sound like music to Xavier's ears rather than a command.

Xavier said not a word.

"Xavier, my love, where are you?" It sounded like a song more than a question.

Xavier still remained quiet.

"X marks the spot over my heart for you. Mommy is sad because she can't find you."

Ms. Venezuela pointed to the cupboard which they both knew was his favorite place to hide and Marquita opened the door to a big smile, loud laughter, and Xavier saying, "Mommy, you found me again!"

"Yes, I did! Now we've got to get Ms. Venezuela to bed."

"Okay," Xavier agreed immediately and stepped outside the cupboard.

Marquita turned back in the direction of Ms. Venezuela and saw that she was slumped in the rocking chair. She screamed. Xavier began to scream too, and he cried because he didn't understand why his mother was screaming. She was smiling and laughing just a moment ago.

Everything changed after Ms. Venezuela died. Immediately, Marquita called her parents and told them that she wanted to come back home with her five year old son but they advised her not to do that. Mr. Miller no longer advised them or gave them notice as to when he was coming to the house; he would just show up. Her parents begged her to stay put because she shouldn't risk being seen and raise any suspicions that she was still alive. It had been five years and a little longer shouldn't make a difference. Not to mention, they had to be on standby to have the house spotless and ready no matter when he would come with more guests, which was more frequent these days.

The ranch was officially hers along with $100,000 US Dollars. Ms. Venezuela's lawyer told her that Ms. Venezuela owed nothing on the ranch and did not keep her money in Mexican banks but wire transferred her money to the US. After she paid him the fees for handling the estate, she was free to do with the money and ranch what she wanted, including selling it or keeping it for herself and her child. The only thing she bought was a car. A small car to get around if she needed to.

Marquita was happy with having somewhere to live, but with no one to share it with or to also enjoy it, the acquisition was great for her personally but emotionally disheartening. It was extremely lonely on the ranch. No Ms. Venezuela or other adult. She had not dated a man in five years. To take her mind off of the bad parts of her life, she decided to focus on educating and train herself along with Xavier as much as possible.

She occupied her days with caring for the ranch. After her chores, Xavier was her focus and she taught him at home all that she knew. She ordered a home study course and completed it in six months. It was a certificate in Information Systems which normally took eighteen months. Marquita remembered that she was always great in school and with nothing but time on her hands, she learned quickly and breezed through the course packet. Fortunately, Xavier was a sponge for learning as well, so he learned about the early days of technology along with his mother.

Four years later, Xavier was nine years old. March 22, 1990.

"Happy birthday to you, happy birthday to you, happy birthday, my Xavier, happy birthday to you!"

"Thank you, Mommy."

The cake was huge and Xavier's favorite. Yellow cake with chocolate icing, nine candles, all glowing, lit up the whole room. Xavier's favorite cake was also Marquita's favorite too. For nine years, there had never been any other children at Xavier's birthday celebrations. This year was no different. Ms. Venezuela was there until he was five and then the last four years, it was only him and Mommy.

Marquita looked at her son eating his cake, the television playing in the background, darkness slowly rolling in to make way for the moon in the sky. She looked at her handsome boy and realized that this was no life for a smart, beautiful boy at nine years old. He must meet children his own age, experience more people and have a life. This was a good life here but no life for a child. There was a whole world out there, and Marquita was going to give it to her son even if she had to risk it all. She made up her mind once she put Xavier to bed and the last dish was washed, just like Ms. Venezuela required each and every night.

The next day, Marquita ordered luggage from the JC Penney catalog. A few weeks later, the bags arrived and as quickly as she took them out of the box, she was putting their clothes in them.

"Mommy, what are you doing?"

"I'm packing so we can go home for a visit."

"Home? We are home, Mommy."

"Not my home. This is Ms. Venezuela's home, not mine. I want you to meet your grandparents and your uncle. We leave in the morning," she explained.

"You sure?"

"I'm very sure."

The next day, up early and ready, Xavier was in the front seat excited about the journey. Marquita locked the front door and headed home.

Once they arrived at the huge house, Marquita had expected to see someone tending the grounds or to see her mother sweeping the grand front porch as always, but there was no one. No one greeted them by waving at the car as it went along the drive way.

She pulled her car to the back of the house near the door of the garage and entered the kitchen. There was no one in the kitchen or the smell of food on the stove. This was very strange and totally unlike the Miller House. Someone was always somewhere doing something.

And then, someone spoke. "I timed it just right. Whose little boy is that?"

"Mine," she answered.

"He'll be mine before we leave here today."

"No! Hide, Xavier, hide and don't come out until you hear my voice."

Xavier looked around and ran as fast as he could to a nearby cupboard to hide just as he had done so many times before.

"He can run and hide, but we'll find him and take him with us. I can tell he's Brandon's by the light hair and eyes. Oh, yes, little hottie. You should have never let my son put his dick in you. Miller blood is running through that little boy and he will be coming with me and not staying in this godforsaken village with the likes of you."

"No, sir, please don't take my baby," she pleaded.

"Too late. I promised Venezuela I wouldn't come on her property for anyone there, but you are not on that ranch. You came on my property. Everything that is here is mine."

"Where are my parents, my brother, Andre and Antonio—"

He cut her off with, "Good and gone. I have a new crew who will do whatever I say when I say it."

"Yes, sir," the very tall black man said.

"You know what to do."

Two men grabbed Marquita by her arms. She kicked but one man grabbed her legs while the other one held her arms. She screamed, "No! I didn't mean to, but I loved him. I really did."

"Bring her here."

They brought her up close to him. He grabbed her face, put his hand over her mouth and continued, "It doesn't matter. Andre should have killed you long ago but he didn't, so now he is dead. Your parents are dead too. As soon as we find your brother, he will be gone, but today is your day. Kill her."

Their grip was too tight; there was no way she could move. They dragged her into the back room where one shot was fired. Xavier came out of the cupboard into the arms of Jefferson Miller.

Xavier screamed, "Mommy, where's my mommy?"

"Dead."

Xavier started swinging his arms to hurt or somehow touch the very large man but he missed with every swing.

"You're a fighter and I like that, but you're not old enough or big enough to fight me." Xavier kept swinging until his shirt came off his shoulder slightly so that Jefferson could see his birthmark.

He kept a tight grip on Xavier and said, "Not only do you have my boy's hair and eyes, but you've got his birthmark as well. My heir."

The two men who had Marquita earlier came back in the main room.

"Tie him up and put him in the car. You gonna have to hold him down cause he's a fighter."

"Yes, sir," the men replied.

They took Xavier and put him in the car, and when they turned back, the house was literally on fire. Xavier screamed through the cloth tied around his mouth, not knowing what would happen next. What would happen to him? Where were they taking him? Would they kill him just like they did his mother? The future was not bright at all any more. The light in his eyes officially went out and he passed out from the trauma of it all.

Chapter 4

The Visitor

"Xavier, Xavier! Where are you, my love?" Xavier heard his mother calling his name. He could see her long, flowing curly black hair and smell the lavender in the air. The game hide and seek was always a favorite of his and his mother. Being an only child, meant all the attention was on him. The love, time and care of his mother was evident. She spoiled him rotten. But who knew that nine years would be all he had with her? He was still a baby, at least still the baby of Marquita Hernandez.

From the sweet sounds of laughter, giggles and play, to the horrible screams of, "No, not my baby! Don't take him! He's mine!" The nightmare of that day haunted Xavier even unto this very day. He woke up in a sweat after seeing his mother in his dreams again. Somehow, he must have fallen asleep on this cold, hard cot, the smell of urine still in the toilet too close for comfort.

"Get up, you've got a visitor. Some high-powered lawyer here to see you," the guard said.

Xavier slowly cleared his eyes and rose up off the cot. He followed the guard down a long hallway. The lock snapped loudly and the door suddenly opened. It wasn't a high-powered lawyer after all.

"How are they treating you?" Brandon Miller asked.

"Why are you here? Is it a holiday or something? That's the only time I used to see you, holidays, back in Lexington. I must not have checked the calendar." Xavier rolled his eyes as he replied, looking at a wrist with no watch still standing at the closed door.

"Sit down and shut up, smart ass," Brandon said. Xavier remembered all too well those staged holiday gatherings with everyone on the land coming to the big white house for dinner. The food was good because Ms. Dorothy, the black maid and cook, did all of the cooking and spent more time with the Millers than she did with her own family. The music was good. The conversation was stiff, as were the handshakes with those small bonuses that were given out before they headed back a half mile down the road to the small white house. As usual, Xavier would hide in the dumb waiter as they called it because Ms. Dottie wouldn't use it. He would hear the conversations that would go on with the Millers after they all left. Those years when he was little, hiding from his mother and Ms. Venezuela, sure paid off.

"How did you know I was here?" Xavier asked, quickly coming out of his daydream.

"I've always got connections and always will. They let me know everything, even out of state."

"I can't believe you would have the nerve to come here. They could keep you here just as much as they can keep me here."

"Don't worry, son."

"Don't call me that! You never treated me like a son and you know it!" Xavier whispered through clenched teeth. His fist balled up on the table but he made no noise. He knew not to scream out loud or pound the table like he wanted to because his stay would be worsened by the outburst.

"You are right, but I'm here now."

"For what?"

"To get you out of here."

"Now, you want to help me? I've been on my own, educating and taking care of myself since I ran away at eighteen. You want to help me now? Why?"

"You know too much," was the answer he was given.

"And? I haven't talked before, why do you think that will change now?"

"They could lock you away for a very long time and force you to talk."

"You think so.

"I know so. The real lawyers will be here tomorrow to bail you out, but you can't go back to your apartment now. It's potential evidence for the case they are forming against you. I've got an apartment already set up and paid for you when you get out."

"Thanks, but just get me out of here and I'll get my own place and pay my own bills. I have for twenty years. I don't need you to pay any bills for me."

"Suit yourself."

Brandon stood and yelled for the guard. The guard was slow in coming so he yelled again.

"One day you're not going to be able to yell for a guard and get out."

"Not until Hell freezes over," Brandon said.

"I think it's starting to get chilly right now."

"You threatening me?"

"No, just saying,"

"Which means nothing from somebody sitting there in day old clothing, smelling like old liquor and bad sex that may soon turn into a permanent orange jump suit."

"We'll see, but the sex was good."

"Who are you trying to convince?"

"Definitely not you."

"Exactly."

They were both lying. Xavier knew it and Brandon probably did too, but they would never admit it to each other. They never had said they loved each other but there was a mutual respect that only two liars, deceivers and two-faced men would know. As much as Xavier hated this man and despised his ways, he knew that deep down inside, part of Brandon Miller was in his DNA and he was his father.

Xavier wondered if his parents ever really loved each other or if it was just sex? That question would be in his mind the rest of his life because his mother wasn't here to tell him.

Just then the door lock popped open. The guard opened the door and Brandon Miller walked out. Xavier smiled to himself.

The next day, Xavier woke from a dreamless sleep to shower and change into that orange jumpsuit he had been dreading.

After a horrible breakfast, the guard rattled his bars and said, "You've got another visitor. You are popular. She's pretty too."

"Thanks."

"You're not welcome."

When the door to the visitor room opened, Xavier was stopped in his tracks by the one face he had dreamed of for years. Standing in front of him, beautiful as the day he met her at nine years old, with the darkest coal black hair, long enough to meet her waist, was Normalinda Martinez. She had on a smoke grey suit that matched her eyes, which was very unusual for a Mexican anywhere.

She was accompanied by an African American man who clearly had a crush on her because he became all about business when watching Xavier's eyes on Normalinda.

"Good morning, Mr. Xavier Hernandez Miller," the man said.

"You can stop at Hernandez, the Miller is totally unnecessary."

"As you wish. We are from Smith & Preston, hired by your father, Mr. Brandon Miller, to represent you. I'm Harold Williams and this is—"

"Normalinda Martinez."

"I don't know who that is, but she is Linda Martin." Williams was slightly irritated and thought, *how does this convict know someone I've been trying to sleep with for three years? Is this why she hasn't gone out with or given me the time of day?*

"Oh, so that's what you go by now," Xavier said with a slight smile.

Linda Martin said nothing but lowered her head and let Harold Williams continue. Xavier could see a small smile on her face that she tried to hide when she bowed her head, but those deep dimples always gave her away.

Xavier never wavered from looking at the woman known as Linda Martin. She stood in front of him, shifting her weight back and forth on those three-inch heels that she must have learned how to wear over the years, because they had run barefoot all over the Miller Lexington Horse Farm. They only wore shoes on Sunday, those staged holidays, or other very special occasions. He knew exactly how her mouth felt and tasted on his tongue as well as every inch of her body. He knew the exact speed to go while making love to make her scream. What they did together was always make love, never just sex, which he'd been having a lot of over the past twenty years or so. Xavier remembered always having to lay a blanket down when they were in the stalls because surprisingly enough, she was allergic to hay and it made her itch. He had an itch he knew she could scratch if she were willing but brought again out of the wonderful daydream, he suddenly heard somebody calling his name.

"Mr. Miller, are you listening to me?" Williams was getting irritated, and so was Xavier.

"No, because my name is Xavier Hernandez and not Miller, no matter what my record shows." Xavier took his eyes from Linda and was staring at Harold Williams whose nostrils were suddenly flaring in heightened frustration.

Linda, knowing that she had to intervene quickly or they would be fighting and this case would be stalled before it started, interjected, "Harold, can you give us a minute?"

"Are you serious?" Harold responded, still staring at Xavier.

"Yes, just give me a minute," Linda said with raised eyebrows and slight head nod.

"I don't know if it is safe," Harold rebutted.

"She's safe, man, just leave us alone," Xavier said sarcastically.

"Who you calling man? Don't let this suit fool you," Harold said with his voice slightly raised.

"I'm not fooled at all. The hole doesn't scare me. If you feel froggy, then leap," Xavier said through clenched teeth.

"There ain't nothing but space and opportunity," Harold Williams said, with his arms outstretched wide extending from his six foot three inch frame.

"Get out, Harold!" Linda yelled.

"I'm going. Guard!" Harold Williams yelled and banged on the door. The guard unlocked the door and escorted Harold into the hallway.

"You are beautiful, and congratulations on becoming the lawyer I knew that you would be."

"Thank you, but we don't have much time. So what's this all about?"

"I really don't know. I haven't even been charged yet. I think I'm here under suspicion of something or other."

"Something or other? Come on, Xavier, you've got Interpol coming at us."

"At us, I like the way that sounds."

"Cut the crap. I haven't seen you in twenty years. What did you do?"

"I didn't do nothing,"

"You did something, for International Police Agents to be traveling across the country and halfway around the world to interrogate you. I'm surprised they haven't sent you away already, but because of your daddy, everything is supposedly held up. We've got police on the way from Louisville, Interpol from DC and Paris headed this way on a red eye tonight for you. What's up?"

"I really don't know."

"You're a terrible liar and always have been. You've got that way of looking down when you're not telling the truth so let's have it. You don't know about which part? What you have done that is making them come for you, or you don't know at all?"

"I like the sound of the second one," he replied.

"Stop. We are getting nowhere."

"Get me out of here. I can take you places and you know it."

"That won't be happening anytime soon,"

"Oh wow, Counselor, you left the door open and I can wait. I've waited this long and you are definitely worth it."

"So you're going to tell me that you've been celibate, waiting on me, when you know exactly where I've been all of this time?"

"No, I would definitely be lying if I said that, but you have always been on my mind."

"Sorry, that was a mistake to go down that road. This is a professional meeting and has nothing to do with the past twenty years. Let's go back. Am I in for any surprises when these people get here?"

"Yes, probably, but we'll both be surprised by what happens."

"I knew it. Let me get out of here."

"Norma Linda, and we know that is your correct name."

"Yes, but I dropped the Norma long ago. Your family advised me to while strong-arming my family after law school. They might have helped me get into law school and get a full ride because the last name Martinez means I'm a minority, but I busted my own ass to study, get through classes, exams, top of my class, law review and this job. I owe your people nothing, but like a ball and chain, rich people never let you forget where you came from. I digress."

"I'm sorry. I see that we've both had to make some serious sacrifices for where we are in life. I get it and know what sacrifice is every day. Oh, and by the way, the view of your ass from here is wonderful."

"Stop it."

"Only if you mean it."

"Stop."

"One question. What's up with the serious dude you have with you? He trying to get what's already mine?"

"Yours? What's yours? I've been taking care of me and mine for twenty years without you and your family's help."

"You know what I meant."

"Yes, I know what you meant and, yes, he wants a chance but I don't date co-workers. I don't date, period."

"Yep, you've been waiting on me."

The room went still as they stared each other down. Each of them had their own memories of how they met, how they fell in love and the heartbreak of separation. How would they move back in each other's lives? Xavier, sitting there in an orange jumpsuit headed for prison, possibly for life, and Linda Martin, standing there in a custom made suit, high heels and a promising future. This was a mess, disaster, and a catastrophe rolled up into one.

"You going to tell me, or do I have to find out on my own?"

"You'll find out when I find out."

"Okay, have it your way, but I'll probably be back tomorrow when INTERPOL gets here."

"I look forward to it."

"Xavier, when are you going to finally live in your truth and stop running, hiding, ducking and dodging life?" Linda said while gathering her things.

"Hopefully soon."

"I hope so too, but I also hope you don't have to be behind bars and can be free on the outside of these walls and the inside of your heart one day."

"I agree."

Linda went to the door and yelled for the guard. The door lock popped and the guard opened the door. Harold was standing against the wall with arms folded, looking extremely irritated.

"You done?" Harold asked.

"Yes, we're done. Let's go." Linda handed him his briefcase and blocked the doorway. Harold was tall enough to see that Xavier was sitting, waiting on the guard, not moving or saying anything. He took the briefcase from Linda and they were escorted out of the door.

The guard said, "Let's go."

Xavier hesitated for only a second before he stood from his chair and headed to the door. He knew what was to come next, the cell and his thoughts. He dreaded it, but there would be no way that he could keep his mind from going back to Lexington, meeting Norma Linda and living with her parents so long ago.

Xavier arrived at his cell and as soon as the door closed, his room turned into a movie theater bringing everything back, from sights, smells, tastes, good times, bad time, voices and choices.

No sleep came. Only the scenes, smells and savory taste of pain, loss and the lack of love, could he remember and see the vivid images over and over in his mind. There are times when you're so tired that sleep doesn't come because the realities of life take over and they are stronger than any ability to doze off, let alone sweet sleep.

Thirty Years Earlier...

"This is where you're going to be living," Jefferson Miller said as the big black car drove up to a small house about a half mile away from the spacious, huge mansion. Xavier said nothing as he looked at the house in front of him. "I've provided the money for food, clothing and your amenities for you to stay with them. They are nice people, loyal, quiet and trustworthy. You'll be fine."

Xavier got out of the car and stood just a distance from a white house that looked like a miniature version of the mansion his grandfather lived in. Jefferson made the introduction but Xavier still said nothing. He did not shake Mr. or Mrs. Martinez's hands but he did eye their two girls and a boy who stood on the front porch in their nightclothes watching the whole conversation. The oldest girl was nine, like Xavier, the boy, a younger version of his father at seven years old but very tall for his age, and the youngest sister was five years of age. The children said nothing but watched every move of their parents and Mr. Miller, who they knew was their parents' boss and the land owner.

Xavier would soon find out that this was one time Jefferson Miller told the truth. The Martinez family didn't know all of the details of why Xavier was here, but the look on his face, they recognized immediately and knew all too well themselves the loneliness, pain, trouble, fear and sadness when they saw it. Over the years, as much as they tried, they could not get Xavier to warm up to them as his foster/godparents. Xavier always called them ma'am and sir which was polite, but he knew his place in their lives and vice versa. They were his caretakers, Mexican as well, but he felt that he was no more than property, a thing or a new acquisition, not by choice but forced upon them by the boss. Xavier could easily blend in, but they weren't his parents. His mother was dead and his father did not acknowledge him.

It was a solid year before Xavier actually spoke. It was Norma Linda, the now ten year old who got to hear the first words.

"You hungry? I found some blackberries," she said while walking along the back side of the farm.

"No," was all Xavier could say.

"Oh my goodness, he has a voice along with that appetite."

"Yes, I have a voice, I just don't use it often. I keep my mouth shut and my eyes open."

"Well, hopefully, you will use that voice in school so you can stop getting a zero for participation."

"I'll try."

"Great, now stop standing there and help me pick these blackberries for Mama to make us a pie."

"Okay."

That was where it all started. Normalinda and Xavier were inseparable. Because Norma was his age and they were in the same class at school, they spent a lot of time together even outside of school. They walked to school together, ate lunch and did their chores together. At school and over the next few years, Xavier would beat up any boys who tried to mess with her or even tried to like her. He heard the boys talk in the locker room after gym class and most of them thought she was beautiful. By middle school, boys were saying not so nice or leud things they would like to do with and to Norma. Xavier got into many fights and a black eye was what he became known for. Surprisingly, he had the evidence of the fight, but fortunately for him, he was never caught and no one ever told on him. He was almost invisible.

All of those fights paid off when he thought his heart would burst the day Normalinda grabbed him by his shirt, pulled her toward him and kissed him when they were cleaning out the horse stalls in the barn at age twelve. Oh, what a feeling. Finally, someone showing him some affection besides his mama, which seemed so long ago. He was a boy so they worked him like a slave, but finally, the feel of Norma's soft, sweet mouth. That taste left on his tongue from the sweep of her tongue in his mouth. The fresh air blowing her dime store cologne in his nose that smelled like early morning rain to him but probably stunk to everyone else. Not to mention her blooming body that was going from girlhood to young womanhood pressed fully against him, which made him hard in places and blush all over in others for the first time. Oh, what a feeling. Young love is precious, priceless, and painful all at the same time. Oh, if he could go back to a time of innocence, simple times and that little white farm house again. Tomorrow was uncertain and what the future held for him was even more uncertain. He must finally decide what was actually important in life. He had missed out on a real, normal family. Normal family, what did that really mean and what does that look like for him? How many hours Xavier slept, he didn't know, but suddenly the pictures stopped and it went black just like the old televisions did back in the day.

———— ЄжӠ ————

The next day after clean-up and a not so appetizing meal, it was time for Xavier to face whatever was next.

"It's time," the guard said as he opened the door and escorted him to the interrogation room.

Chapter 5

Mouse

When the door opened, there was an unexpected visitor standing in the room. Because he could trust no one, Xavier said nothing until the door slammed behind him. He knew that his visits were being monitored and anything said in the room could and would be used against him.

"Who are you?"

"I'm here to represent some interests that concern you and me. Please sit down."

Once they were both seated, both of their voice levels lowered and their mouths barely moved.

"What in the fuck are you doing here, Mouse?"

"Trying to get you out of here."

"By perpetrating as what? My lawyer, a friend. or the snitch we both know that you are?"

"Listen, X, you know I ain't no snitch."

"Then why are you standing there in a suit and I'm here in an orange jumpsuit? Pizza Man? Mouse or Rat?"

"Listen, we had to get you in here to protect you."

"We? Who is we now, Mouse? From what? I been holding myself down, running, ducking, dodging and taking care of me as well as covering for your ass for twenty plus years. I am ready for this shit to finally stop. When is it really my turn to stop hiding like a criminal and be able to live my life, whatever the hell that looks like to me?"

"I get it. I came early to let you know about the two sets of people coming your way. They are coming from Paris to actually bail you out. Take you to the safe house in the area so they can finally bust the big guy."

"Really? I've heard this before. I've testified, went under, laid low, connected to the goods and the creator and here I am, still in the slammer."

"It's about to be over."

"When?"

"Soon."

"While he is eating Ruth Chris, I'm eating hash. I just want a life. I don't even want my life back because I didn't like the old one I had and lived. I just want to build something without looking over my shoulder. I thought your ass was dead with that one shot shit."

"No, just trying to get you safe."

"Okay, who comes first?"

"Annette and the crew from Indiana."

"Why? She's had enough problems. That's the reason why I left town, to let her be happy, and then I thought I could try to start over. What I didn't count on was her inventions and how valuable they really were and seemingly still getting more valuable as we speak."

"You got that right. The bad guys still want them but the good guys, whoever they really are, want everything to be squashed, pay her off so she can live. If things stay as they are, she may be dead before she gets the patent application ink dry."

"Patent, how do you know about the patent?"

"Look at me."

"Never mind. Really, I don't think she'll go for the payout, but we'll see."

"The Paris crew is next, and I've got to get out of here before they arrive. I'll be back when they bail you out."

"Bet," Xavier said but deep down was confused and thought, *how is Mouse going to get back after I am bailed out?*

They finished the conversation with some round and round conversation that no one would understand but the two of them, and then Mouse left.

When Xavier got back to his cell, he realized he had to think and think fast. The cell turned into a movie theater again, playing back the last training mission before it all went south.

"Ladies and gentlemen, trust no one. This is hard for me even to say, but it is the truth. Trust no one but yourself. There are double agents, paid off agents, would be agents, and gone bad agents who may try to set you up. Be aware of their every move and yours too. Be sure to control the situation as much as possible. Never tell your every move to anyone."

Instructor Jones was what they called him and what was on his badge, but what his real name was, they would never know. He was killed two weeks after that session and the body was never recovered. There are no funerals in this business, just missing people. When they disappear, it might be temporary or it could be for life. After seeing Norma Linda, he wanted to try to make a life with her. He looked for her in every woman he met and slept with. None compared. You never forget your first.

So thinking back to Mouse, was he friend or foe? Enemy or confidante? Amazingly enough, Mouse knew all too many details of the itinerary of everybody coming to visit him, who was scheduled to bail him out and where the safe house was. Too much information as far as Xavier was concerned.

"Guard," Xavier yelled.

"What?"

"I need a phone call to speak to my lawyer,"

"It happens in ten minutes after she clears. She's on her way in. I just saw her on the monitors with her fine ass."

"That ass is all mine."

"In your dreams."

Xavier said nothing but kept his eyes fixed on the door and when the guard would let him out.

Minutes later, "She's in," the guard said with a smirk on his face as he turned the key on the heavy metal door.

Xavier still said nothing. When he arrived in the interrogation room, she was alone and Xavier was thrilled. "You came alone."

"Yes, I thought you would tell me the real deal if I were alone. Also, Miller said that I should be assigned as your lawyer alone, without Harold."

"I guess that is one thing I can thank him for."

"Yes."

Xavier and Normalinda sat down at the table across from each other.

"You know we are not alone in this joint. I need you to get me out of here."

"If I do, where will you go?"

"I know a place, but I need to get out of here and I'll tell you everything. I'm going to need your help moving forward."

"I have to let Mr. Miller know about this if I am going to get you out. It's his contacts."

"I don't care about him or his contacts, but if it gets me out of here before Interpol shows up, that's great."

"Why don't you want to see them?"

"I can't tell you right now, but I will. It's going to take Heaven and Earth to get me out of here but know this—I was always taught that you should control the situation as much as possible. I had a visitor earlier and he told me too much about everything. That, to me, tells me that he is probably working on both sides of this situation. I can't fall into the wrong hands. Understand?"

"I understand, but if you're trying to con me, I'll never forgive you. You hurt me once by leaving."

"I never lied to you."

"Yes, but you never told me the truth, either. Why did you leave, anyway?"

"I can't talk here, but I will tell you. I promise."

"This is clearly your last chance. Agreed?"

"Agreed."

"It'll take about two hours, but I should be able to get you out. The judge has already signed the papers to release you, but you can't run. You can hide but you have to stay in town."

"Can you make it an hour? I feel like company is coming sooner than two hours."

"I'll try."

"That's all I can ask. By the way, you look beautiful."

"Thank you, but we don't have time for that right now."

"There's always time for that."

"You haven't changed. Still the same Xavier, eager and hungry. It's never enough." Normalinda stood, collecting her things.

"When it's good, it's good."

"Shut up. Guard!" Normalinda yelled as she banged on the door.

Meanwhile, a black Tahoe was sitting on Interstate 71, exactly forty miles from Cincinnati, Ohio. Detective Peaches Simpson and Special Agent Ben Walker, along with Duane and Annette Jackson, and Hank and Jasmine Simpson, were along for the journey.

"What is going on?" Detective Peaches asked a nearby highway worker when they pulled to the emergency lane.

"An oil truck has turned over, spilled its oil in the road. It's burning and blocked all of the lanes going Northbound."

"Are you kidding me? We are on police business. Can we get into the emergency lane and go through with our lights?"

"No, because the entire highway is on fire, ma'am, and we all have to wait."

———————⬦⬦⬦———————

Simultaneously, the Paris transportation workers had gone on strike. That happened often in Paris. One minute, the planes were ready to take off and the next minute, they were grounded and no one was going anywhere until the dispute was settled.

Agent Ferre'asked the ticket agent, "How much longer before the plane will take off?"

The young woman rolled her eyes, shrugged her shoulders and said, "You will know when I know."

The line of travelers behind him groaned loudly. Some stayed in line to make arrangements for new connections because they knew they had already missed their connections in other airports. Others sat down in disgust or went to the bar to have another drink near the gate.

Ferre' turned to Puchini. "I guess we get there when we get there."

"Correct, but how will we get a message to Miller and X?"

"Technology is wonderful," Ferre' replied with a smile.

Two hours later, Normalinda showed up just like she promised.

"How did you get me out?" Xavier asked as they walked down the courthouse steps.

"Don't ask, and I won't tell."

"You're right, I don't want to know."

"Where to?"

"I'll drive," Xavier said as Normalinda pitched him the keys.

"You can't leave the state."

"I won't. Nice car."

"Thank you."

"A long way from the Ford minivan your parents had," he said.

"The one the Millers gave us to drive because they still owned it."

"Never knew that part."

"Of course, you didn't. You were in your own world, trying to just get through each and every damn day."

"So you did get me, for real."

"Yes, I did, and know that rich folks always going stay rich."

"You are right about that. You need something from your house?"

"No, I have all I need in the trunk."

"Wow, a woman prepared."

"I have to be. When I left the courthouse with you, I became a marked woman."

"Miller has got you, and so do I."

"Maybe, maybe not, but we'll see after you tell me what this is all about."

"I will but much later."

"We probably only have about twenty-four hours."

"Why?"

"They are going to come for you no matter what. According to the news, there is a major fire on I-71, but it won't burn forever. Paris has delayed flights, but they won't be delayed forever, either. You've got forty-eight hours max before all hell breaks loose."

"That's fine. That's all the time I need."

"I hope so."

For the next twenty-five minutes, they drove in silence to smooth jazz playing on the radio. They were headed to a seven-story building on the city's north side. It was in an industrial park, in clear view for all to see and definitely not what Normalinda considered a safe house.

"This is the safe house?"

"Yes, just wait and see."

"Okay, if you say so."

When Xavier drove up to the gate, he placed his face in front of a screen and the electronic voice said, "Welcome back, Mr. Miller."

"Mr. Miller? What happened to the name Hernandez?"

"When it is necessary, I will pull it out in a heartbeat. Miller bought me the building several years ago. I renovated and upgraded it about five years ago but have never lived in it until now."

"Oh, really."

"Really."

When the outer gate opened, he drove about a quarter of a mile to the building, and when he placed his face against the screen again, the doors opened to an elevator and they drove right in.

"Xavier—"

"Just wait."

"I'm waiting, and I am trying not to freak out."

"Don't freak out, just relax. It's going to be fine."

Xavier pushed the button to seven and the elevator lifted to the seventh floor. When it stopped, they got out of the car, emptied its contents and he opened the door to a spacious condo with ever amenity.

"This is beautiful."

"I'm glad you like it. I built it for us."

"Why?"

"Because I've always had you in my heart and in my sights. Miller is my father and I will have to live with that the rest of my life, but I must make some changes. Somehow, God allowed me to reconnect with you and I'm never letting you go."

"So you wanted to be captured?"

"Definitely."

"This is a fortress and it would take an act of God to get in here."

"Exactly."

"So why?"

"Not until after showers, food, wine and conversation, will I tell you. Ladies first. Follow me."

Normalinda followed Xavier to a large, beautifully decorated bedroom with an adjacent equally huge bathroom with shower, hot tub and all of the modern conveniences. Somehow, there was a walk-in closet on the opposite size of the room that was filled with clothing from casual to formal. How he knew her size, she would never know. Most Mexican ladies increase in size as they get older, but Normalinda never did. She was still the size ten that she had always been.

Everything in Xavier wanted to go into the bathroom and get in the shower with Normalinda and she probably wouldn't resist, but he owed her more than just great lovemaking; he owed her an explanation. So he went to the opposite end of the condo to his own bedroom to shower, change quickly, and start dinner.

While Normalinda heard the pans clanging and the music playing in the background, she made a quick call.

"Hello."

"Hey, Papi, how are you?"

"I'm fine."

"Everything all right there?"

"Yes, you coming to see me soon?"

"Yes, in about a week or so. I love you."

"I love you more and miss you."

"I miss you more. See you soon. Kiss everyone for me."

"I will."

Normalinda quickly hung up the phone but Xavier heard the whole conversation. He designed the condo so that he would know everything going on in it. It was the agent in him that caused him not to trust. They drilled it in him and it latched on, and he was sure that it would never let go.

When she came into the kitchen, he had to ask, "I thought you said you didn't have a boyfriend?"

"I don't."

"Who was the call to?"

"You'll find out as soon as I find out what's going on with you."

"Fair enough. Red or white wine?"

"Guess."

"Red or dead."

"How do you remember that?"

"I remember everything."

The intensity of Xavier's stare caused Normalinda's body to catch fire and it started from her head down to her toes. She dipped her head like normal and Xavier knew that he had touched her core. She always dipped her head like that when she was embarrassed, trying not to laugh, collecting her thoughts or aroused. Xavier went back to cooking and turned his back on her so he could collect his own thoughts and not ditch dinner and make love on the floor. She was on his turf, in his sights, and more importantly, within reach. His hands would stay firmly on these pots and pans rather than come across the counter and have her for dinner instead of the seafood and pasta.

"You're still a fan of seafood, right?"

"You remembered."

"I told you I remember everything. It's nuts and strawberries that you're allergic to."

"Right again."

Normalinda wondered how he could have a fully stocked kitchen and refrigerator here when the address where he was arrested was on the other side of town. She watched him skillfully cook, turn each entrée, and coordinate the whole meal totally without her help.

"You're very handy in the kitchen. No wife, no kids, never married?"

"No."

"Have you ever wanted that life at all?"

"Yes."

"Then go for it."

"I'm trying. Doing my very best."

Xavier could see through the stainless steel refrigerator that Normalinda bowed her head again. He knew he was getting to her. Hopefully, she would fully yield after this meal and a transparent conversation.

"Do you mind setting the table?"

"Don't mind at all. Where are the utensils?"

"Everything is in the pantry. I haven't filled the cabinets yet or the drawers. They remain empty until I really move in all the way."

The table was already covered with a beautiful cloth to match the kitchen and there were two candles, but it was still too early for them to be lit.

Xavier set the food on the table and it smelled delicious and looked as good as it smelled.

"Wow, shall I call you Chef Xavier now?"

"Nope, just cook to survive. I picked it up overseas and loved it. I figured if I ever fell out of love with technology, I'd start cooking."

"Well, I will look forward to the taste test."

"Okay, let's stop talking about it, sit down and let's dig in."

They sat in adjacent chairs. Normalinda did the sign of the cross over her food but Xavier said, "Give me your hand."

Normalinda blushed slightly and put her hand in his.

"God, we thank you for this day, opportunity, food, and most of all, Normalinda. Amen."

"Amen. I didn't take you for the religious type."

"I'm not, but my mom taught me to pray and I've needed to pray so many times, I can't count anymore."

"That's so good to know."

Xavier said nothing in return but saw her dipped head again and the slight smile. It made him smile too. They made small talk about the meal and the the day but held off talking about anything related to the case until after dinner. The dishes were washed and the towel was put on the handle on the stove when they looked at each other in silence, with only the music playing.

"It's time," Normalinda said.

"Yes, it's time and I'm so glad that we're alone and I can talk to you on my turf."

They headed to the couch and sat opposite each other.

"Let me say this. I'm hurt, confused, and disappointed, but I just need to get an understanding of the why, the contributing parties, and what I'm about to face," she began.

"Fair enough." Xavier took a deep breath, turned off the stereo, and began. "It was Spring Break. I had turned eighteen the week before and was happy to be off from school. I knew that I had to make some decisions about my life because staying in Lexington was not an option for me. Old Man Miller had big plans for me, but I wanted nothing of it. He never told me in person and out of his own mouth what his plans were, but I heard them through the dumb waiter."

"You were in that thing?"

"All the time."

"Ms. Dorothy warned us never to be in that thing."

"Did I ever listen to anything anybody told me?"

"No, but it was dangerous in there."

"I survived. Can I finish?"

"Yes, but that gives me shivers just thinking about it and the danger."

"I appreciate your concern, but it was a risk I was willing to take. Anyway, Brandon Miller agreed with everything Old Man Miller said. I don't know how it happened, but the old man began to cough. The more he coughed, the more he begged Brandon for his medicine. Brad didn't get it to him. He let him just gasp for air and his breath."

"He let him die?"

"Yes, Brad never called the ambulance until it was over. I heard the whole thing. I never saw anything, only heard it. After he was dead, Brad called the ambulance and screamed for the help to come quick."

"We never knew that."

"Of course, you didn't, and I didn't know really what happened after that because I ran. I ran as fast as I could, to get away from there. If Brad Miller would let his own dad die, where would that leave me?"

"Nowhere."

"What he didn't know was that I had enrolled in an electronics school in the Silicon Valley area that recruits for the military, etcetera."

"How did they not find you?"

"I changed my name and created a different license. Remember when I came to Lexington?

The old man just gave me to you guys and that was it. I had no birth certificate or anything. Do you know how many people are smuggled into this country and in those horse carriers/transports each year?"

"Hundreds of thousands," she replied.

"Exactly. I didn't come on a commercial plane with a passport. I was flown on a private plane onto private property. Miller property. So after school, I joined the military, special forces. Do you know what that means?"

"Confidential information, spying."

"Yes, and somehow they traced me back to Lexington and Miller. I have a rare blood type."

"AB Negative."

"How did you know that?"

"I think I saw it on Discovery Channel one time," Normalinda said but she dipped her head oh so slightly.

Xavier knew there was more to her answer, but he didn't press her on it because this was his time to come clean and not to interrogate her. "Okay. Anyway, there are so few of us in the US that they all have to be recorded and, remember, I did fall out of that tree when I was twelve."

"I still have the butt scars from that because I was standing there and didn't talk you out of it."

"It wasn't your fault and I'm still sorry about that whipping that you got. I never wanted you to be in trouble over me."

"Too late for that. They talk about black mothers and whippings, but Mexican mothers can get your behind too."

"True. Moving on."

"Yes, moving on."

"While in the military, they are always keeping an eye on suspicious activity overseas as well as in the States. The Miller farm was one of those places that they were watching all of the time. They knew I was connected, but I always used your parents' name instead of the Millers. That way, they wouldn't realize that I was related and just consider me just a farm hand. I downplayed my connection because I'm Mexican. They know that Mexicans are illegal a lot of the time, so they don't ask too many questions but want loyalty. I was loyal. I learned everything I could. I was good with math, technology and everything else. I was athletic then and still am now. My biggest problem was that people were always trying to set me up or double cross me. I already had trust issues but that didn't help matters."

"Why are thy coming for you?"

"See this bracelet here?"

"Yes."

"Annette created it to help find missing children and those taken in sex trafficking. It was supposed to be financed by Brandon Miller, but he was double crossing her and selling it overseas to people who were unscrupulous and literally evil. They had plans to use the inventions for their own agenda and not the big picture. The idea was for me to get the plans. They were going to kill Annette, take the inventions and make billions, literally."

"What happened?"

"Too many players, too many double crossers, too many double agents and too much money involved. It's hard to tell who is telling the truth and who is lying."

"How do you know you can trust me?"

"I never would have brought you here if I couldn't trust you."

"But how do you know?"

"I don't know for sure. I am taking a chance. Risking it all but that's life and love, isn't it?"

"Yes, it is."

"So why haven't you taken a chance and loved?"

"Hell no, we are changing the subject. This is all about you and what I'm about to face. I have risked my career, family, life and everything to even take this case and to be here right now. I could have easily put you in an Uber or taken you to a car lot. I didn't have to come here with you."

"Now you know why you're here."

"I get it, but why is Annette coming here?"

"Because she wants to slap me in my face and/or find out why I double crossed her, she thinks."

"Why is Interpol coming?"

"They either want to kill me because of all I know, or they want me to go into hiding so the bad guys don't kill me, but I think there is a mole on the inside."

"A double agent?"

"Yes."

"So you're running from everyone."

"Yes and no," he answered.

"Yes?"

"I needed to clear my head, get on my turf so I can get myself ready. They came for me prematurely," he explained.

"How do you know?"

"Sometimes I just know in my gut that someone pulled the trigger too early because I was so close to completing the assignment and getting the bad guys, but now I feel like I'm back to square one."

"That must feel terrible," she sympathized.

"Damn right. I have a life invented in my head that I want, but this move right here has seemingly moved it further and further away from my grasp. Not to mention Miller."

"What about Miller?"

"He is my father by DNA, but I've never felt like a son and he is a criminal, ruthless and a killer but still my father. How am I supposed to feel? I was cramped in that damn dumb waiter to be near someone who has part of them inside me. I hated him and his father for how they treated my mother and myself, but I hated myself for wanting to be near them. I could have run away at sixteen, but why did I stay? I really didn't want to run at eighteen, but I was finally an adult, sort of, and could run and he could do nothing about it. I was finally free, but was I really free?"

"Freedom, what is it, really? I worked hard, got through school, had a..." Normalinda paused slightly.

"Had a what?" Xavier asked and knew that she was keeping something from him and if he was honest, so was he.

"Had a hard time with it all and would love to move on with my life, but now I see you again."

"How does that make you feel?"

Normalinda reached her hand to his across the couch as a symbol of understanding, but just their hands touching was still magnetic. Their hearts, memories and experiences were reconnected by that one touch. Tears began to stream down Normalinda's face. "I missed you so much after you left. I know we were young and most people discount young love, but it was serious to me. I felt lost. I was hurt because you didn't take me to the prom! I had to go with safe and rather round Manny Garcia. Don't you dare laugh."

Xavier smiled just a little. "I'm sorry."

"I'm serious. I was angry and I was confused, but I had my family and had to build a life as best as I could."

"What did you build?"

"Hard work, a degree, financial security, love from my family but that's it. I didn't have that security like my parents. When they go to bed at night, good or bad or an ugly day, they have the comfort, safety and security in each other's arms. I don't go to bed at night with my bank account but alone, with only my pillow and blanket."

"Norm, me too. I haven't slept in twenty years."

"Wow, I haven't heard that in twenty years. No one calls me that."

"But me, and you're hearing it now. I've been training, running, hiding, dodging people, lying and praying to get out of every scrape and situation, just to survive. I haven't been able to really rest in years."

"That's no life."

"Exactly." Xavier moved closer to Normalinda on the couch, their hands still in each other's grasp but still not close enough for Xavier.

"How do I know that you're not trying to trick me right now?"

"What is your heart saying?" he asked.

"I can't really trust my heart. I did one time and it was broken," she replied.

"By me?"

"Yes, by you."

"Anyone since?"

"You've asked me before but, no, because I wouldn't allow it."

"Why?"

"I tried a few dates and even slept with a couple, but it didn't work. Don't look at me like you've been celibate all of this time."

Xavier rolled his eyes and couldn't begin to count all the people he had slept with. "I confess that I have not been celibate, but they weren't you. Those guys didn't look like me and those girls weren't you. They didn't smell, touch or taste like you or me." He was wide awake and the wine had worn off long ago. He looked Normalinda directly in the face and said what was in his heart, "I'm here now."

"Yes, and I think it's time for me to take advantage of something I want for a change."

"Normalinda, There's nothing stopping you but space and opportunity."

Normalinda giggled so slightly, whether being nervous or excited about what would come next when she rose up off of the couch and straddled his lap for that first kiss.

Xavier kept both arms on the couch to give her full access to his any part of his body that she wanted and he loved every second of it. He did not put his hands on her body at all for the first few minutes because he wanted her to set the tone and speed and allow her to give him instructions and directions to please her to the maximum. She deserved this, and he owed her that.

"Too many clothes," she said as she took her t-shirt top off over her head. She was normally in suits and stiletto heels but was comfortable in her lounge wear. When the top came off, it revealed two beautiful, full breasts that she positioned directly at Xavier's mouth. Only a thong and his thin shorts separated them both from heaven. She did the old school 'clothes burn' but Xavier's manhood rose to the challenge while straining against his shorts.

With only his mouth, he sucked each one until she screamed even without his hands on any part of her body. Between his mouth celebrating her breasts and his manhood getting teased by her grinding against him, his mind was screaming and his body was on fire. Just think, in the past, there had been so many women he had slept with when he'd almost called out Normalinda's name at climax that it scared him. She was here now and he couldn't say anything. He didn't even moan or groan from the pain and pleasure of it all as he feasted on her. He could freely say her name now, but old habits die hard.

"Please touch…"

She never got the last word of 'me' out, only another pleasure-filled scream as his hands lifted her up off the couch, but not away from their heat, to the floor. Gently, they landed on the soft carpet and her thong was ripped off and his shorts flew off to who knows where. He knew she was wet but wanted to make sure by dipping his tongue inside her. He brushed her clit and she screamed again. When he finally entered her, they both let out a loud, "Yes!" in harmony.

Her next word was, "Faster."

Xavier happily obliged her request and drove in deeper and faster. It was his pleasure and her pace that drove them both over the edge.

He thought his weight was too much and lifted up slightly to disconnect but Normalinda said, "No," again.

With a few more kisses and hands gently caressing each other and being massaged in the right place and this time at their own pace, their lovemaking started again. Like hungry and ravenous people, they loved each other. Tasting, sucking, licking and grinding to their hearts' content from one end of each other to the next. It had been twenty years since they had made love and their tastebuds had seemingly missed and needed to get reacquainted with every texture of their bodies. The third time was in the shower, with the multi-directional water massaging their bodies as Normalinda took Xavier in her mouth and made him scream her name over and over again. The fourth time was in the kitchen while snacking on each other with syrup, fresh fruit and more wine to gain strength. If that weren't enough, the final time was in Xavier's California King-sized bed in the position they loved best, with Normalinda on top, grinding to her heart's and body's content.

"Aren't you sleepy yet, lady?"

"Exhausted, but if I go to sleep, it'll be morning and I don't want this to end," she answered.

"I understand."

"Are you going to ever stop looking at me like that?" she then asked.

"Like what?"

"Like I'm dinner and you're hungry."

"Right now, I'm famished for you now more than ever."

"I'm glad and it feels so good to be wanted for the right reason."

"What reason is that?"

"For me. To love me only, I hope, and not what I can do for you or help you with."

"I understand the hesitancy, given the situation, but right now I'm going to need your help legally and that's it. I've been pulling my own weight for a while now. I can get a job if I need to but I don't need to. I have plenty of businesses and flows of income, so I'm straight."

"We drove into this building so you know I wasn't talking about money," she said.

"I'm sorry, but I had to say it just in case that beautiful head of your thought it."

"I thank you, but I'm worried and also a little sad."

"Why?" he asked.

"Where will this go? You've, no, *we've* got so much going on that I'm hoping we don't just have this time and then you're gone again for twenty more years. I can't wait another twenty years."

"I'm fighting like hell to not have that happen again. Especially now that I've made love to you as a grown man and not as a curious boy. I can't get enough of you and want you more and more."

"That's nice to hear, but I still feel like you're hiding things from me."

"I am," he admitted.

"What have you left out?"

"A lot, and for good reason."

"Why? So you are still lying to me!"

"No, calm down, Norm, I am not lying. I just can't tell you everything. It's for your protection!"

"So you're going to let me go into a courtroom or out of this building in the morning, blind?"

"Not blind, but I only suspect who the real double agents are. But I'm not for sure. They will reveal themselves in time, but I can't worry about that right now. I just want to be with you."

"I want that too, but I have to keep my wits about me and be ready for what's next," she reminded him.

"We're never really ready for what's next. We just have to go with the flow. Right now, you are assigned as my lawyer to uphold the law in Ohio. Where else are you licensed to practice?"

"The tri-state area, Kentucky, Indiana and Ohio."

"Good."

"I'm not running," she told him.

"No, we're not running. We're still in Ohio, but just in case they push me or drive me or take me into one of those states, I need to know I've got back up from someone who really cares about me."

"I do, but your father—"

"Don't call him that! Just say Miller for now, okay?"

"All right, Miller is not going to let you go anywhere where he doesn't know about it."

"So, how loyal are you to him?" Xavier's mood was suddenly broken and he sat on the side of the bed with his back to her at the thought that she could be telling Miller everything.

"I work for the firm. Miller has always wanted me to just work for him, but I can't do that. I have a lot at stake and can't risk it for him and being on his team. He has somewhat of a say on what I do because he is the firm's largest client."

"Wealthiest, you mean."

"That too, but also the dirtiest."

"You can say that again," Xavier agreed.

"I have seen him in action. He will move Heaven, Earth, Hell, and the demons to get what he wants."

"But he has to be stopped."

"Is that what you're assigned to do, stop him?" Normalinda asked.

"I've been trying for twenty years, but he always gets out of it."

When the Louisville crew finally arrived at the police station, Peaches said, "You all stay in the truck. Ben and I are going in to check on the status. If you're able to see Xavier or speak to him tonight, I'll call you. It's late, but we'll see."

They exited the vehicle. Annette said, "I just want this all to be over with. Why would Xavier double cross me like this? I trusted him."

"Babe, it has nothing to do with trust but with evil, greedy people; it has to do with money and power."

"Say that again. Peaches says this goes high up, so we don't know who all is involved. I just want all of us to have regular, safe lives again. Whatever that looks like. We have been back and forth for years, with people trying to destroy us for too long," Hank said.

"I agree. Eventually, this must stop for all of our sakes," Jasmine added.

Chapter 6

The Louisville Crew

When they arrived at the receiving desk, the desk officer asked, "How can I help you?"

"I'm Detective Simpson and this is Special Agent Walker, we're here to see Xavier Martinez," Simpson said, both showing their ID badges.

"Yes, we've been expecting you but you're too late."

"Why?"

"He was released by a judge's order and to his lawyer four hours ago."

"Released? How?"

"Ma'am, all we have are the signed orders and the paid fine. We don't make or control the rules, you know that. We can only enforce them. The court date is scheduled for Tuesday morning at 9:00. If you want to see him, you'll have to wait until then."

"Who is the judge?"

"Judge William Smith III."

"Smith, dirty as they come."

"I heard nothing, ma'am." The officer never looked up from the paper on the desk.

"Sorry, thank you for your help."

They moved away from the desk and headed outside. Their next move was to sit and wait for Tuesday. They checked into the Courtyard Marriott hotel on the Kentucky side, in Covington. It was cheaper but right by the highway and just minutes from the courthouse. Ben and Peaches stayed in connecting rooms and the other two couples were in adjoining rooms as well. It made communication so much easier.

Hank and Jasmine knocked on Duane and Annette's door. They all sat around on the chairs and couches, and Duane and Annette were on the king-sized bed.

Annette had set up her laptop and they were all still wide awake from the trauma of the drive up. A normal hour and a half drive had turned into six hours.

"So, Peaches says we have to sit here and wait until Tuesday, right?"

"Correct, but that still doesn't mean we can't poke around and see what's going on in the cyber world."

"Babe, you're the tech genius. What do you propose?"

"I want to see if Xavier's bracelet is still connected. He used to wear one when we were in beta test mode."

"Well, is it?"

"Give me a few minutes to check. Yes, it's connected and still working, but he hasn't pushed on yet."

"Is there a way to push on from your side?"

"Of course, there is, my wife's a genius," Duane said.

"Thanks, babe, but, yes, there is a way and here we go now."

Meanwhile, in Miller's penthouse suite, his phone rang.

"Louisville is here."

"Did she come alone?"

"No, she's got company, but I don't know whose side he's on."

"Well, we've got to make sure they both are on our side."

"Will do."

The phone went dead and Miller went back to watching the game. His plan was coming together rather nicely.

Xavier saw his bracelet light up and so did Normalinda.

"What's happening to your bracelet? It just lit up."

"Yeah, I saw it too. Annette must be trying to contact me. She is the only one who can do that with her laptop and through her system," he explained.

"What can it do?"

"You can two-way communicate without getting on a public server. Let me push on."

Normalinda sat in awe and watched the whole thing.

"Hello, Annette. This is Xavier."

"Hello, Xavier," Annette replied.

"Xavier, you snake, if I get my hands on you, you will wish you never knew me!"

"Hello, Duane. You have every right to be mad, but let me explain—"

"I don't want no explanation, I want—" Duane was suddenly cut off.

"Hush, Duane. Where are you, Xavier?" Annette asked.

"I'm fine, Annette, but are you alone, with only you and Duane?"

"I see that you're avoiding my question but, no, we're not alone. Hank and his wife Jasmine are here too, but you can trust them."

"Are the detectives or the police reps from Louisville with you now?"

"They are in the hotel but not in the room with us now."

"I need you all to listen and listen carefully. You can't tell anyone, not even the police who brought you, what we're about to discuss. Everyone agree?"

"Agreed," they all said in unison. Duane rolled his eyes, but he was too curious to mess this up.

"First, Annette, I apologize for the lying and deceitfulness, but it was for your protection."

"I knew it. I knew that slick dude was lying."

"Shut up, Duane, and listen."

"I just want everybody to know I was right."

"Okay, you were right."

"Secondly, I care about you deeply, Annette, and want nothing to happen to you but I don't know how much I can protect you anymore. To tell you the truth, as much as I can is what I owe you at this point. I have been an agent with the International Police or Interpol for years, trying to take down these bad guys. They are big time human traffickers. Your invention has threatened to stop their operation, find the missing and return them back home. They couldn't have that. It goes high up. The only problem is that the bad guys still want to sell off your invention and use it for other ways instead of saving kids. There are literally billions of dollars involved, politicians, judges, Internationals around the world who want the patent for themselves and they want you gone. Do you understand?"

"Understand, but what happens next?"

"Several things. I don't know when I'm going to meet with my Interpol contacts, but somebody may be a double agent and try to kill me. I suspect that somebody with you could be dirty too. I suspect that somebody in Cincinnati's police could be dirty and my biological father is somehow involved as well. I don't know fully all of the players in this game, but it's dangerous. Is there a way to get away from them?"

"Probably not, because we were told to sit tight until Tuesday."

"Annette, do you have extra bracelets with you?"

"Of course."

"Make sure the four of you have them on and activated. We never know what could happen next."

"Great idea."

"This is what I think you guys should do next," Xavier said and mapped out the plan for them to follow.

Duane, of course, was hesitant, but they really didn't have a choice, did they? Had Peaches gone bad? Who was Ben Walker, for real?

There were too many people, too many opportunities to take advantage and the saying goes that 'everyone has a price.' The other side of that coin is whether you're willing to pay the price and what are the repercussions of the price paid?

Only time would tell.

"I've held up my end of the bargain so far, haven't I? So why are you coming at me like I'm going to cave or get scared or something? You make sure that you do what you said and don't screw me!" Peaches yelled as she pressed end on her phone.

Suddenly, there was a knock on her connecting room door.

"Come in, my side is open," Peaches said with another yell.

"Peaches, you're yelling so loud. Are you trying to tell everyone in the hotel what's going on or what?" Ben gently scolded.

"No, I'm just frustrated and angry."

"About what now, Peaches?"

"The plan is not coming together as it should."

"Of course, it's not. Xavier's not stupid and the other people we are working with are not stupid, either. There is a high price to this game and I hope you're still okay playing it."

"I guess I am."

"Guess? What the hell! A lot is riding on this and your job is just the tip of the iceberg. Our lives are literally on the line for this case. You can't fold now, we're almost to the end, tying up all the loose ends and, hopefully, getting a good night's sleep for once."

"You're right."

"I know I'm right, but what you need right now is a drink, a shower, and me. In that order." Ben took his voice down low, just the way Peaches liked it.

"Who you ordering around?"

"You, and you love it," he replied huskily.

"I didn't say I didn't like it, but where are the drinks?"

"Right in my bag."

"Your shower or mine," she asked next.

"You pick. I'm ready when you are."

"Oh shit, I just got hot. Take off them sweats, Daddy, and I'll meet you in my shower."

"Now you're talking,"

"You guys got the plan?"

"Yep, we are good," Annette said.

"Did you all bring a lot of luggage?"

"No, just backpacks, so we are good."

"See you soon."

"Annette, you really trust him like that?" Jasmine asked.

"Girl, I have to at this point. I don't like the idea of not trusting Peaches or using you for bait, but right now, we don't have a choice. We can sit here and do nothing, or we can be ready. Hank, you in?" Annette asked.

"I guess, but Peaches is family," Hank exclaimed.

"I know, but everyone has a price. Who knows if he's right, or if it's a trap, or if he's trying to get the invention for himself or what."

"I can activate any device from here, but I didn't bring everything here with me. The invention is not on me; it's safe for now," Annette said.

"As far as Peaches goes, Hank, if she's on the right side, it won't matter. She'll be fine and we will too," Jasmine added.

Just then, Hank's phone rang.

"Y'all tucked in, or do I need to come in and see?"

"Peaches, we doing what grown ass adults do."

"Great, goodnight, and we'll meet in the morning around ten for breakfast. I'm exhausted and hit the mini-bar, so I'm not good for anything right now."

"Enjoy, Peaches, and goodnight."

Hank hung up the phone. "Sounds like we're good, no matter what we do."

"Right," Duane added.

They quickly began packing their bags, alerting no one. They headed down the back stairwell because Peaches and Ben's room were near the elevator. When they got to the bottom floor, it was the loading dock. Just like Xavier said, about an hour later, a white delivery truck showed up. On the side of the truck, it said, "Hernandez's Tacos." When the door opened, Normalinda was standing there, Xavier was driving, and they were both dressed in shirts labeled, "Hernandez's Tacos." As the door closed, Xavier sped off again to the safe hiding place.

Chapter 7

Who is Telling the Truth?

It was extremely risky for the four of them to leave Peaches because she was family. Hank had known her all his life and she was the police, but what was Xavier, really? He had lied and almost gotten Annette killed. Duane was sure of it, but what now? Who were they to believe? Like Jasmine said, if Peaches is clean and honest, then it'll be fine and she'll eventually forgive them. If not, they were safe, or were they?

They arrived at Xavier's hideaway on the lowest floor in the garage. He got out of the truck and opened the sliding door for them to get out and they all stepped out carefully, looking both ways.

"Where are we, man?" Duane asked.

"My house," Xavier answered.

"House? It doesn't look like a house to me," Annette said.

"It'll make more sense once we go upstairs. Grab your bags and let's go inside. I'll introduce you all to each other once we're inside."

They all grabbed their bags, following Xavier toward a door but when it opened, it was an elevator. He pushed the button to seven, and they climbed to the top floor. When the door opened, they were in the living quarters of the building, overlooking an industrial area. It wasn't busy because it was Sunday evening and shut down for the week. In the morning, it would be busy with commerce.

"Come in and have a seat. You all thirsty?"

The four stood close to the elevator, not knowing what to expect. Xavier was moving closer to the kitchen. The floor plan was clean, white and silver/stainless steel, and wide open except the bedrooms.

"Yes but thirsty for answers more than anything else," Annette added.

"Well, first, sit down. Let me introduce you to my childhood sweetheart, Ms. Normalinda Martinez. We've known each other for years and now she is my lawyer," Xavier said with a smile. He was hoping to put Duane's mind at ease that any feelings he had for Annette were over.

"Hi, I'm Linda Martin. Most people in the area do not know me as Normalinda Martinez, just Linda Martin," Normalinda stated.

"You trying to hide something, Ms. Martin?" Duane asked.

"Just call me Linda. No, it was just suggested to me to change my name once I left law school," Normalinda stated.

"Trying to hide your heritage?" Duane asked again.

"No, just bettering my options," Normalinda added.

"I get it. Don't like it, but I get it," Duane said.

"So now to the business at hand. Annette, your invention has caused a lot of people to want what you've created. The problem is that these people are criminals and don't play fair. Eventually, Peaches is going to find out you guys have left and all hell is going to break loose. I am scheduled to appear in court on Tuesday morning at 9:00. I suspect that neither side wants me to appear in court, INTERPOL or the Police. INTERPOL and the police departments normally work together to catch criminals and INTERPOL provides international information, but neither of those sides want to catch criminals as much as they want what you've invented. I don't want what you've invented. I am striving to expose the bad guys on the inside. I've been working for

INTERPOL Internal Affairs as a special agent for twenty years."

"So that's why you were working for me, or with me," Annette surmised.

"Exactly. We got a tip that you were in danger and that the Metro Louisville is a major transportation station or human railroad for human trafficking, just like it was a major area for slave trade back in the 1700 and 1800's. Back in the day, it was the Ohio River. Right now, it is I-65, which is a major highway from north to south. It's all still going on now but not with just a few tens of dollars, but millions of dollars. But if your invention is on the market publicly, kids can be found and that business will be shut down."

"That was my point."

"It was a great idea for the kids and women being held and traded but not for the business and sick people buying and selling them for sex and other activities. Do you know that there are more than horses in horse trailers and definitely more than products in eighteen-wheeler trucks that transport all day and night?"

"Crazy."

"You've got that right," Xavier agreed.

"We've also been tipped that Louisville Police has cops who are involved."

"Peaches?"

"Never."

"You suspected me, right?"

"I guess, but Peaches is family."

"I understand Familia, but everyone has their price. I suspect that they were planning to hand you over to someone to get you to either talk or steal the technology from you. My job was to flush them out, but it all got shut down when LMPD showed up."

"That's what that was all about a couple of years ago."

"Exactly. The plan is to get the insiders on this level and then go for those at the top. But in the meantime, your inventions are not safe, and neither are you, until these people are arrested. What were Peaches' instructions to you guys?"

"Stay put and go nowhere."

"Where does she think you are now?"

"In bed, not coming out for the night and we'll meet at ten in the morning for breakfast," Annette said.

"Great, we will keep it that way for , but see if she cancels on you in the morning, and then that will tell me a lot. Turn off ringers and trackers/mapping on your phones, just put them on buzz."

They all put their phones on mute and, as always, Duane needed help turning the map track off on his phone. He was the most technology challenged of the group, but Annette was helping him greatly in all areas of his life, including technology.

"I have everything you need. Help yourself to the food in the fridge, pantry, etcetera. I have plenty of bedrooms to sleep, and each one has its own master bathroom. If for some reason, I have visitors, you will need to exit through the closets in your bedrooms to the next floor down. If you're in the kitchen, that pantry doubles as an exit as well."

"This is some real 007 shit right here," Duane commented.

"Thanks for the compliment, Duane, but he was a fictional character," Xavier said with a chuckle.

"Fictional character, my ass. I know that dude was for real."

"Whatever. Just remember that I'm on your side but have to play both sides to get to the bottom of it all. I don't know who'll show up tomorrow, so be ready. Any questions?"

Hank and Jasmine quickly undressed in their room and climbed under the covers to their safe place to talk.

"What do you think, Ja?"

"I don't know, babe. We're here as support for Duane, but why would Peaches let us tag along if we were in danger caused by her? Wouldn't she try to stop us at all costs?"

"Right. But she knew she couldn't stop me for sure, with Duane along too," Hank replied.

"True, but Peaches has been on the force forever. Why would she go bad or rogue when she just got promoted? Have you ever known her to have money issues?"

"Yes, she had trouble right before Mama died, but Mama helped her tremendously. I remember because Mama asked me if she should give her the money for her backed up mortgage. I said sure, but Mama died before she could make the first payment and I just wrote it off."

"Interesting. Well, Hank, you know I don't like to waste any time that we have alone without the twins. We have this big old bed with these beautiful, designer sheets. What should we be doing?"

"Girl, you ain't never, ever got to ask. Come on, vanilla thunder, let's make Mama scream."

"Yes!"

Annette and Duane were settling in for the night as well.

"So, you've been kind of quiet, 'Net, what's on your mind?"

"Everything. I'm scared to death. I was just trying to help somebody with this invention, not get myself killed."

"I know, but I'm here. Xavier sounds like he's for us and I don't want to believe that Peaches is bad, but who knows. LMPD hasn't been getting good press in a long while."

"Exactly, but I just want to help somebody and hopefully make some money. My business was going so good."

"I know, babe, but let's get this over with and, hopefully, you can get back to doing what you love. Maybe I'll find what I really love doing as well. In the meantime, I'm here and love you more than you know."

"Babe, I feel it and I know it. Know that I love you more. Let's see if we can get some sleep."

"Come here."

"Gladly."

In each other's arms, Duane and Annette tried to get the comfort that they both needed.

On the other side of the condo, Xavier and Normalinda were wrapped in each other's arms as well.

"So, what's the real plan?"

"Look at you, girl, trying to second guess me."

"Xavier, I don't know you, but I know you. You told those four nervous people the basics but didn't give them all of the information they needed to know, and that includes just how much danger they're in."

"You're right. Do we have to talk about this now?"

"Yes, because tomorrow is another day, and it'll be another surprise for Normalinda, and I don't think my heart can take it."

"Okay, let's make love one more time, and then I'll tell you," he suggested.

"Nope, because you're going to go really hard to make me drop off into a sex coma."

"That was my plan, but spoiler alert, you ruined it,"

"Spill it," she said.

Xavier smiled that sly smile that made most women weak, change their mind, and give in, but Normalinda won this round by getting out of the bed, sitting in a chair while crossing her arms to make sure he knew that she meant business.

Xavier actually did spill the tea on the plan for the next day. Tuesday was the court appearance, so Monday was wide open with plenty of opportunity for things to happen that would change even more situations on Tuesday.

Way across town, it was late, but Peaches and Ben were on speaker phone with their contact.

"It's a simple process. We'll bring her to you and hand her over. You put the money in my account and we'll part ways, just like that. They're here with us in the hotel, safe and sound."

"Bitch, you had better not be screwing around with us."

"Why would I do that? I'm not going to be your bitch too many more times."

"You're still a cop and dirty, but we really mean business. There is money to be made. You will get your share, but the natives are getting restless."

"It's been too long for me too. You act like I ain't risked nothing."

"Well, whatever. All I know is it's time to settle up and stop dragging your feet. Remember, you mess with us, people can and will come up missing. You got it?"

"Who you threatening?"

"You, bitch."

"There is a cap coming straight to your ass. You hear?" she threatened.

"Try it, and we'll see whose ass has a cap," was the reply.

"Shit, what time?"

"Ten, at the place. I'll text you."

"Bye, bastard," Peaches said.

The phone went dead and Ben went off, "Who the fuck he talking to?"

"Me, but he's already gone so we have to make other arrangements for the kids tomorrow."

"They are fine right here. They ain't going nowhere but sightseeing. The Aquarium is down the street and the Underground Railroad Museum is across the bridge, with all of the food they can eat that can be delivered."

"Yeah, you are right."

"I know I'm right. Get your fine ass over here for one more round before I go to sleep."

"You so nasty."

"You ain't seen nothing yet."

Chapter 8

Monday Moves

Just like Xavier said, Hank's phone buzzed at 9:00 a.m. and he looked at the name on the screen, dropping his head because he knew who was on the other end of the phone.

"Peaches, it's too early." Hank didn't have to pretend because he had been asleep. He and Jasmine's lovemaking last night was not only love but desperation, reassurance and connection to each other, which right now was the only thing that was making sense. Everything was still a mystery.

"Hank, you guys will have to fend for yourselves today. I've got some meetings to attend. I'll catch up with you guys later on tonight or first thing in the morning."

"Cool. We are adults and can take care of ourselves. You be safe, hear?"

"Got it, cousin. Love you."

"Love you too."

Hank hung up the phone, and Jasmine said, "I guess we've got our answer."

"Yep." Hank rolled over toward the wall because he didn't want Jasmine to see just how hurt he was by Peaches' phone call.

Jasmine didn't need to see his face. She rolled toward him and hugged him tight, to let him know that it wasn't his fault, that she had his back now and always, and that Peaches was making her own choices.

At 11 a.m., they headed to the kitchen to see what smelled so good.

"Come on in," Normalinda said.

"What smells so good?"

"Xavier has stocked this refrigerator with everything I need to make breakfast tacos. Anybody allergic to anything?"

"Just hunger," Duane said.

Everybody giggled and started filling their plates with tortillas, meat, eggs and grilled vegetables.

Suddenly, an iPad on the counter began to ring. Normalinda answered, and they saw Xavier's face.

"Where are you?" she asked.

"Don't worry about where I am, but can everyone hear me?"

"Yes," they said in a chorus.

"Good, because this is a preliminary meeting and you can hear everything, but they can't see or hear you."

"Who are you meeting?"

"You'll see. Here they come."

A large white truck arrived at the garage. The door slid open and out came Peaches, Ben, Mouse, and Harold, but a long black limo came up just a few seconds later. Out of that limo, stepped Brandon Miller.

"So, y'all ready?" Brandon asked.

"Been ready," Harold said.

"Do you have the package, Peaches?"

"Sitting tight," she answered.

"We could have made the transfer right here, but I guess it'll be cleaner tomorrow," Brandon said with a smile.

"Yes, tomorrow is much better, at the courthouse."

"Who is your friend, Peaches?"

"Just call him Ben," she said.

"All right, Ben. I hope you know the deal and how it is about to go down."

"I do," Ben said.

"We ain't getting married. We making money here."

"So with him added, is the price still the same?" Harold asked.

"Hell, Harold, is that all you are worried about?"

"Hell, yeah, Mr. Miller."

"You've been paid before and you'll get your cut this time too."

"Thank you," Harold replied, satisfied.

"Mouse, you and X are awful quiet."

"I just want it over with. This took too long," Mouse said.

"Me too," Xavier said.

Normalinda wondered, *where is Interpol? When will they show up?*

Just then, a white Escalade drove up and two men got out.

"Oh hell, here is the calvary come to save the day, I guess," Miller said.

"No, Mr. Miller, we haven't come to save the day but want to join the party. We got held up by the Paris transportation union, but we're here now. Who are all your friends, Miller?"

Xavier thought, *Hold up, they called him Mr. Miller. Something's fishy. They are about to ruin everything. Join the party? I thought they were here to stop the madness.* Xavier simply watched because he didn't know these agents at all and suspected that they were either not still with INTERPOL or working for Miller himself. This scene was getting more complicated by the minute.

"Who the hell are they?" Peaches asked.

"This, my dear, is the International Police, or Interpol. Agent Ferre' and Agent Puchini are here to be the mediators for our International customers. They have no real jurisdiction in this part of the world, they're just here to make sure their representatives' interests are carried out."

"This just gets dirtier by the minute."

"It takes dirty to know dirty," Miller told her.

"Shut up."

"Stop it, kids."

"Do we really need these other two people? The pot is already being cut so many ways. Do they get a cut of it too?" Harold asked.

"I'm about to shoot you myself, Harold, so you will shut the hell up."

"Well, I'm just saying."

"Stop saying anything!"

So Miller knows everybody who's here. That means he set up the whole thing. Me getting arrested, the fake INTERPOL agents, Peaches, Ben, Mouse and Harold, are all a part of his plan. If any money goes anywhere, it will go with Miller. What kind of father do I have? Xavier thought.

Back at the condo, Hank could say nothing. He left his plate, threw down his fork and pushed his chair away from the table. With long strides, he went into the bedroom where he and Jasmine had slept the night before. He couldn't listen to what was going on any longer.

Duane followed him to the bedroom and saw him looking out the window. "You okay?"

"Hell no! How could Peaches be involved in this? She was going to just turn Annette and her invention over for money? She has a job, a career, and just got promoted. Why? I don't know what to believe any more."

"Me, either! I'm just as angry, especially seeing as you trusted her and have for years and then I've trusted her with my life!"

"Now we have to put our lives and our women's lives in the hands of a relative stranger, Xavier, who probably has more identities and lives than a cat."

"I know, but what else is there to do?"

"There's got to be another way out! D, we've come too far. I've got Jasmine and my two babies to think about, not only just you and Annette. We need this finished and settled."

"I told you not to come. You guys can get a car and go home now and leave the situation."

"Nope, not without my brother and Annette."

"I appreciate you being my ride or die, but this shit just got really real," Duane said.

"You telling me."

<hr>

"Jasmine, can you come in the other room with me?"

"Sure."

When they both entered the other bedroom, Annette closed the door. "Now Duane and Hank are scared and angry, but we have to figure this out logically."

"Okay, my first thought is that Xavier was the problem, but really, Peaches may be the sell out."

"Correct, but I still have the information, the inventions, the beta tested jewelry, the application for the patent, etcetera. They can't get anything done without me," Annette reminded her.

"I think that's the point, that they want you, to get it out of you by torture or any other means. Where is everything else?"

"In a secure lock box at the bank. I am waiting on the patent application to be completed within the next thirty days."

"That's what they want right there, the patent!" Jasmine said.

"So the only way to get to it is through me, or to do something to someone I love so that I'll turn it over. Xavier came the closest, and Duane only knows certain parts of it. I had to search for years for an attorney legit enough to handle the application."

"Right. So, that means you and Duane are in the most danger in this process and probably why Xavier brought you here."

"So the objective all along was to bring me here."

"Probably, but how will they get the rest?"

"That's what still baffles me," Annette said.

"Me too."

Four hours later, Xavier came in. Everyone was in their separate rooms, including Normalinda.

"Can everyone come out here please?" Xavier yelled from the kitchen and self-made meeting and community room.

"What the hell was that about?" Duane screamed as he walked out of his room.

"Calm down, Duane. Everything will be over tomorrow. Let's have a seat," Xavier said.

"Really? How do you figure?"

"Just have a seat."

Duane plopped down hard on the beautiful white couch, with Annette beside him. The couch was big enough for them all to sit on it, but only Hank and Jasmine joined them. Normalinda and Xavier were in the two black chairs facing them.

"I know that you guys heard all of what was said," Xavier began.

"Most of it until I could take no more," Hank told him.

"Well, you know that there a lot of players in this game, but the bad guys from the good guys are still not known."

"How is that possible? They were all there. How did they know about the meeting if they weren't involved?"

"Miller called the meeting. I was there to see who would come besides me. That means he has influence, connections with everybody. The two INTERPOL guys are actors, I believe, and not really a part of the agency," he explained.

"How do you know?"

"They called him Mr. Miller."

"And?"

"If you work with him closely, you normally call him Miller only and not Mr. Miller," Xavier said.

"Harold calls him Mr. Miller."

"Harold must be a kiss ass or a brown noser."

"Wow, I haven't heard that word for a long time."

"Well, I don't care, but that's what he is and if he is trying to take what's Annette's, I think he needs to be shot," Duane said.

"Babe, calm down."

"I don't want to calm down. I just want all of this shit to be over, go home and enjoy our life and cut out all of this shit."

"I totally agree ,but it's not over until the arrests are made, which will happen tomorrow. I recorded everything and the FBI has the recording. They have had more information that I can remember but have never had all of them this close and you here too," Xavier told them.

"So I'm the bait," Annette stated.

"Exactly. No one's going anywhere until they can be assured that the patent has been turned over, sold, or the invention's mass produced, sold and the money split. There is upfront money for getting the patent and then there's production money on the back end."

"For my hard work," she said.

"Yes. That's how criminals work. They let somebody else do the work and then the only work they do is figuring out how to get it from you."

"Why didn't they do all of this when the police or whoever came for me two years ago?"

"The invention worked and it worked on you. You had tested it out but the patent is even more valuable than the invention itself," Xavier explained patiently.

"So they let me wait. Came after you, set you up to get me involved, which in turn brought the invention to them one month before the patent is granted," she replied, fuming.

"Correct."

"What time does it all go down?

"We leave here at 8:30 and go into the back way of the courthouse. Peaches thinks she isbringing you to the courthouse, but I have you with me instead."

"Who knows the plan?"

"Only me and the FBI," he said.

"Nobody else?"

"Nobody else."

"If anything happens to Annette, I will kill you myself," Duane said very calmly and quietly.

"I'll give you the gun," Xavier said.

"Deal."

They all left to go to bed and face whatever would happen tomorrow.

Each couple in the condo, as well as Peaches and Ben across town, were holding each other tight under the covers, but sleep was not coming easily. For each of them, tomorrow held its own problems, concerns and uncertainties. Would they live or die? Would they even walk away without a scratch? Not one of them knew the answer. Tonight, was all they had so they made the most of it. There is a hunger, drive, pull and tug of love or lust when you face death. The consummation and the connection are wilder, rougher and faster, in an attempt to make the feeling more powerful and somehow last longer. The kisses are wetter and the tongues go deeper in every portal of the body to engrave and/or tattoo the taste of your lover on your mouth as well as your brain. What makes people do what they do in spite of the love that they feel for another person? You don't want any of it to end, be over or cease, especially not by death. So what do you instead? You hold on, let go of any inhibitions, allow the tears to fall where they land, as long as you ride your lover all night until dawn. There is the solution. Ride it out until dawn. Giving love a chance to take you there and with every ounce of strength that you have inside and out. In the morning, you may be tired, but you gave it all you had and that is always time well spent.

Chapter 9

The Showdown

Peaches called Hank and asked, "Y'all ready?"

"Yep, we'll catch an Uber and meet you there," he replied.

"Meet me there? We riding together."

"Not this time, Peaches. Not this time."

"Fuck, something's wrong?"

"What, Peaches?"

Only half dressed, Peaches ran down the hall to the room where Hank and Jasmine were previously assigned and kicked the door in. Fortunately, the room was not occupied, empty and clean to prepare for the next guest.

"Let's go, Ben!"

Xavier drove to the courthouse alone. The FBI escorted Duane, Annette, Hank and Jasmine in an unmarked black cruiser. The plan was to come together in the back, under heavy security. Xavier had handpicked the agents himself.

———————⊱⊰———————

Normalinda drove one of Xavier's many cars to the courthouse. When she arrived, Harold was getting out of his car at the same time.

"Wow, new car, and where the hell have you been all weekend?" he asked.

"In my skin, where do you think?"

"I've been texting all weekend and Monday but no answer." Harold opened the door for Normalinda and when she came closer, he sniffed her twice and continued, "Your pussy is still smelling from fucking a certain convict all weekend long, and we feeling ourselves today. Stella got her groove back."

"First, I wash everything on me at least twice a day. Second, you mad cause I never gave you none of this and you've been using your wild imagination. Finally, that's none of your damn business, but since you up in my business, add front, back and from side to side, now."

"I deserved that, but I'm still co-counsel with regards to this case, and you know it. We are shutting it down today," Harold replied coolly.

"What case, and what *we* are you talking about? There is no case as far as I can see."

"How you figure?"

"Sit yo black ass there in that chair and ride shotgun. Don't you say a damn thing. Oh, and furthermore, watch and learn, fool," Normalinda said, putting him in his place.

"Wow, there is a little Latin hood down in there."

"Don't try me."

"Oh, he put it down that good."

No reply from Normalinda, just a side eye that told him everything he needed to know.

Xavier arrived at the table at 8:45 and sat in the middle of Normalinda and Harold. He smelled as good or better than he looked. He turned to Harold first and greeted him, "Counselor."

Harold replied, "Convict, or should I say conspirator."

"Those are your words of choice today?"

"Take it or leave it," the man said.

"What I want to do is take you outside and give you a good ole-fashioned ass whooping, but you're not worth it," Xavier returned.

"Whatever," Harold replied.

"Gentlemen," Normalinda's one word stopped all of the banter.

Xavier leaned toward Normalinda close and whispered, "Hey, gorgeous."

There weren't many people in the room by design and because of the nature of the case. She still whispered her reply, "Handsome sir, you're about to take my breath away."

"That's my goal, but let's get this done first, and then I think the shower, the floor and then the bed this next time."

"As you wish." Normalinda did a slight curtsy and bowed her head in response.

Xavier wanted to scream in laughter and then make her moan and scream under the desk but that fantasy would have to be lived out somewhere else and at another time.

Next to enter the courthouse, was Peaches, along with Ben. To say that Peaches was fuming when she came into the courtroom, was an understatement. The four were sitting together, with Annette and Jasmine in the middle, and Hank and Duane were flanking them on both ends. The

FBI agents who brought them in were seated only a few feet away.

Peaches sat strategically behind them so she could make sure they heard every word she said. Ben was seated behind Peaches instead of next to her.

"Where the fuck y'all been?"

Known of them said a word.

"Oh, so no words for Peaches, who's had and held down y'all's asses for thirty plus years. We'll see who has nothing or something to say after this shit goes down in here."

The next to arrive was Brandon Miller, then Mouse, followed by the FBI members, along with Agents Ferre' and Puchini, who entered last.

The U. S. Marshall came to the center of the room and announced, "Welcome to the U. S. District Court, with the Honorable Judge Smith presiding. All rise."

The judge walked in, sat down, told Xavier and his attorneys to stand and proceeded to read the charges that had been brought against him. He added that, "Based on the evidence that I received on Monday, all charges against Xavier

Hernandez are dropped. Case dismissed." He slammed the gavel down on the desk.

Xavier and Normalinda said in unison, "Yes."

The judge exited quickly and the Federal Marshall locked the door behind him.

Hell broke loose just after the door was closed. Peaches pulled out her gun with her right hand and grabbed Annette by the neck with her left, literally pulling her over her seat.

Xavier pulled Normalinda to the chairs that were behind the desk on the prosecution's side of the courtroom. There were no people there so she was safe. Hank pulled Jasmine immediately to the floor.

Although Duane tried to pull and get Annette from Peaches, she was too strong and fast. He stood and slowly began walking toward and approaching Peaches just on reflex, to knock her down, but the gun was still pointed at Annette's head.

"Get back, Duane. This is what we came for, right here. What's in her head. Unlock the doors and let me leave here with the package I came for."

Annette screamed and said, "Let me go! Duane, Xavier, Hank, somebody help!"

Peaches was always a big woman, strong and could take down any man. "Bitch, nobody can help you now, while I got this piece to your head. If I can't get it out of your head, I'll blow your brains out."

Ben, who had already drawn his weapon, suddenly pointed his gun directly at Peaches and said, "Drop the gun and move away from her now!"

"You ratted me out, Ben? After everything we have been through together? I thought we were in this together. So, I'm taking the fall by myself. You would make love to me and then turn me in? You bastard!"

"You had to be stopped, Peaches. You had to be stopped!"

"Ben, that was the deal you made, to turn me in? That's what you were on the phone about last night? How could you?"

She was still holding on to Annette, who was yelling, "Let me go! Let me go!"

Peaches turned to everyone in the room, dragging Annette along with her, and yelled as loud as she could, "Do you know how little a cop's retirement is? It's $2500 a month! That's all. I'm sorry, Hank. I will always love you! I really needed it this time, and Big Mama couldn't help me," Peaches yelled.

All guns had been drawn out of every holster or hidden compartment that they could find. It was either going to be Peaches or Annette.

Hank had raised his head only to see Peaches with her gun still to Annette's head. Jasmine never raised her head, just kept it down at Hank's request, but she kept praying. Duane stood boldly next to his seat, never taking his eyes off Annette and Peaches as she was slowly heading toward the door.

"Drop it, Peaches!"

"No, I'm not going to jail!" Peaches let Annette go and she dropped to the floor. Peaches pointed the gun at her own head and pulled the trigger. Nothing happened.

"I took the bullets out," Ben said as he and the other U. S. Marshall wrestled her to the ground.

"No, no!" she screamed all the way out of the courtroom. Up until that moment, no guns had gone off.

In all of the commotion, Mouse had crawled toward Harold, who was under the desk. He said, "You're under arrest too, Harold."

"What the hell?"

"Put your hands up where I can see them."

"For what?"

"Conspiracy to commit criminal acts. You're as dirty as I am."

"Not when you're undercover, you're not."

The eyes were off Brandon Miller, so he tried to make his escape through the judge's chambers.

"Freeze, Miller!" Agent Ferre' said, miraculously losing his French accent. There were only three U. S. Marshalls in the courtroom by law. The other two were helping arrest Peaches, but there was only one left.

Miller grabbed his gun from the back of the marshall and pointed it toward his head. "I'm not going to jail, either. I've been through too much to go down without a fight."

"Dad, don't do it!" Xavier said.

Normalinda had never heard Xavier call Miller his dad before. It was a first, at almost forty years old.

"Son, I can't do jail. I'm not cut out for it," Miller said.

Why, in that moment, Miller finally acknowledged his son, none of us will ever know.

Xavier was slowly walking toward Miller to stop him in some way. "Dad, we can work it out. You'll have to do jail temporarily, but you can get a deal. I know you can. You always do. There are higher ups you know who can help get the sentence reduced, so put the gun down. I'm here for you. In spite of everything that you've gone through and what we haven't done together, we can do this together and I promise you, with everything that is within me, I'll try to fix it."

"You can't fix it."

"Let me," Xavier said.

The gun went off and Miller dropped to the floor.

Xavier rushed to his father's side, screaming, "No!"

"No!" Normalinda screamed at the same time. She had hated this man, but in spite of it all, he had helped her realize the life she now could live freely. She was somehow reconnected to the man she'd always loved by the horrible, criminal and devious actions of the man who now lay in his own blood on the floor.

Xavier embraced whatever parts of his father that he could. There was blood on the door, the wall, as well as the floor.

The ambulance and police sirens could be heard ringing louder as they got closer outside. No matter the hate, hurt and loss, Miller was still Xavier's father and he continually cried loudly, "No!"

Xavier clung to him just like he had been the best father ever. It didn't matter if that were not the case because Brandon Miller's blood still ran through Xavier's veins.

When the EMTs came into the courtroom and examined Miller briefly, he was pronounced dead. The courtroom now was officially a crime scene. No one could leave nor the body be removed until the Cincinnati Police, along with the FBI, could determine next steps.

Xavier sat for hours in his bloody clothing and stained hands, answering questions with a blank stare on his face. Normalinda was still officially Xavier's attorney so she was with him the entire time. Hank, Jasmine, Duane and Annette just sat dumbfounded by all that had occurred that day. A day that none of them would ever forget in spite of what they had been through.

Weaker vessel my ass, the women had to be strong for the men. Xavier, Hank and Duane walked around like zombies so the women took the lead on this one. Xavier rode in the car with Normalinda, while Jasmine drove Xavier's car home from the courthouse. They made sure that no one was following them and took multiple exits and pathways to get back to the safe house.

Finally, hours later, they all walked into the safe house, which by now had turned into a grieving station. The each walked in silence to the meeting room in a daze.

Xavier broke the silence first and apologized repeatedly while thanking them intermittently and then apologizing once again. He was running merely on raw emotions. So much to take in all in one tumultuous day. No one corrected, agreed or disagreed with anything that he said, especially not Normalinda. They each had their own journey of emotions to sift through.

Hank had somehow lost his friend, family and foe all in the same day. He couldn't think about having any contact with her ever, in or out of jail. He still had Jasmine, shaken but whole and alive.

Duane would not go five feet away from Annette. He realized that he'd almost lost her today. She was the bait for the whole case, but to him, she was and is the love of his life.

What was left for each of them only time would tell. Would the invention get patented? How long would Peaches be in jail? What to do with the remains of Miller? What about all of the possessions of Miller's? Did he include Xavier in the will at all? Would Xavier be an outsider, a work hand, a pawn or result of a week's love affair eternally? The biggest decision they had to make tonight was who was getting in the shower first and what nightclothes to put on. After that, it would sort itself out in the weeks, months and maybe even years to come.

The next morning, Xavier went to the basement for a swim. It had always been his safe place to gather his thoughts and recoup.

When Duane came to the kitchen, Normalinda was there with coffee.

"Normalinda, where is Xavier?"

"He downstairs swimming."

"Thank you."

"Duane, I don't think he really wants to talk," she said.

"He doesn't have to say anything. I just have to say something to him."

"Be gentle," she pleaded.

"It's nothing like that."

"Okay, then."

When Duane got off the elevator, Xavier was swimming full speed back and forth in the pool. He sat down in a nearby chair to watch and wait for Xavier to finish or at least stop.

When Xavier stopped, he braced himself on the side of the pool where Duane was. "So do you want that gun now or later?"

"Nope, I just came down here to thank you for everything. You saved my love's life. I admit when I'm wrong. It takes me a minute, but I realize that I'm man enough to do it," Duane said.

"You're welcome. Things didn't quite turn out like I thought, but you realize that it is far from over, over, right?"

"Yeah, that's why I was coming to talk to you. What is next? Are there more people coming for her?"

"Probably, how many and when, I don't know. Just like Peaches was enticed by money, there are others who will be attempting to do the same thing."

"But I want us to live and not always be running, hiding and living in a safe house like this. This is nice, but is this a way to live?"

"No, but it's what I signed up for when I was trained to be an agent," Xavier said.

"What about Normalinda?"

"I love her. No lie. I thought that love was lost forever, being undercover. I'll admit, I did have real feelings for Annette. It was probably more protection than anything else, but Normalinda, it's the real thing."

"Then it'll work out," Duane assured him.

"You think?"

"I know so."

"So what's next for you, Duane?"

"A baby! As hard as I went last night, she has got to be pregnant," he replied.

Both men laughed out loud, harder than they had in a long time.

"Don't leave without saying goodbye," Xavier said.

"We won't."

"I'll be up in about ten minutes."

"Take your time and do you."

Finally, an impasse had been reached between the two. Friendship would come much later, but bond, connection and experience would tie them together for life.

When Duane came back upstairs, there was an unofficial women's meeting in the kitchen around coffee and bacon. He knew he shouldn't intrude so he went to check up on Hank.

He knocked on the door and Hank did respond, "Come in."

"Hey, buddy, how are you hanging in there?"

"Not good, but I will be," Hank told him.

"I know this one is hard, but we'll make it. We did with that crazy bitch girlfriend of yours back then, and we will this time too," Duane said.

"Yep. How are you?"

"I'm good. I talked to Xavier and thanked him for everything."

"Look at D, growing up," Hank teased.

"Shut up. I've got to. That's my world sitting in that kitchen. I didn't really want to leave Peaches and the hotel, but now I am so glad that I did. She could have gotten Annette anytime. When they went in the women's bathroom along the way, or any other time. Why wait? Why in the courtroom?"

"I don't know, D, but I'm glad she waited. We really didn't give her much chance because we left. Just in time, but thankfully safely."

"Yes, we're safe."

"For now."

"So what's next, Normalinda?" Jasmine asked.

"Trying to move forward with my business life," Normalinda replied.

"I get it. The big law firm not looking so good right now?"

"Nope. I'm going to need some more time off. Too much has happened. I only know this one thing, and that is that I love Xavier. I always have and always will."

"Glad for you. There's nothing like good love. I have it with Hank and pray for you to get it and keep it with Xavier," Jasmine said.

"I know I have it with Duane. It took a minute, but we're here. My problem is figuring out how to stay safe. I'm going to have a bruised neck for a while from Peaches' grip," Annette piped in.

"Girl, we couldn't even grab you and stop her because she grabbed you so hard and fast. She caught us all off guard."

"I was too far away. I couldn't help nobody but myself."

"Will this ever be over, over?" Annette asked.

"Probably not. There will probably always be somebody wanting what you invented, Annette."

"Well, until then, this coffee and bacon has helped me," Annette said.

"Well, I know that we're not sisters or even friends yet, but there is certainly a bond through this pain and tragedy that will last for a long time," Normalinda said to the other two.

"Let's make sure of it."

"Always."

Xavier came out of the bedroom and all of the luggage that they had was packed and ready to go. How they would get home, they hadn't figured that out yet.

"Y'all ready to go?"

"Yep."

"First, before we go, I have to thank you all for everything. I provided you each a bracelet just in case, earlier, at Xavier's request. Your safety is a priority for me now, so I want you to keep them. I'll make more."

"Yes, baby, you will. Millions more," Duane said as he held her close to him.

"We'll see about that," she answered him with a laugh.

"Xavier, take us to the airport and we'll rent a car there to go home," Duane said.

"Nope, take one of mine. I insist. The Escalade is full of gas. Enjoy! We'll come down to get it in a few weeks. I have plenty of vehicles."

"I see," Duane said, amazed.

"Duane, you drive."

"Gladly."

"One more thing before we go. I greatly appreciate all of your hospitality in spite of the awkwardness. Jasmine, I put extra bracelets in there too, two kids' ones for the twins, and two for your parents. Just to say thank you and, of course, for your protection."

"Thank you, Annette. I appreciate you both," Jasmine said.

"Thank you, love," Normalinda said.

"This is so mature. No cat fights?" Duane asked.

"No crazy. We are all adults here," Annette said with a smile.

They had a group hug in the garage, a little awkward for them all but genuine, nonetheless.

When Hank and Jasmine arrived in her parents' house, the twins ran toward them so fast, it literally knocked them down on the floor with hugs, kisses and loud screams of 'Mommy and Daddy.'

Jasmine could see that Hank lost it for a minute but gained his composure while hugging them both so tight while still lying on the floor.

"So you both missed us?" he asked.

"Yes, terribly."

Jasmine's mother said, "Hank, them five year olds are strong as two baby oxen."

"Yeah, but they mine."

"They sure are." They all laughed.

Jasmine said, "We have a surprise!"

Hank yelled, "Who's ready to go to Disney World?"

The laughter, screams, excitement and yelling of 'yes' carried on for several minutes. The adults smiled and so did the kids.

Annette and Duane arrived in their house to peace and quiet.

"What's first on the agenda, Annette?"

"Meet me in the shower and I'll show you," she said with a grin.

"Girl, stop playing with me."

"I'm not playing, and if you're too slow, I'll start without you." Annette took off running up the stairs.

"Oh no, you won't. Not without me," Duane took off after her two stairs at a time.

Epilogue

Three days later, Brandon Jefferson Miller was buried in the family vault on the farm in Lexington, Kentucky. Normalinda accompanied Xavier through the whole process as his lawyer and love. Surprisingly enough, Brandon left everything to Xavier. The land, cars, plane and any money were his.

Over the next three months, Xavier went through some intense therapy. As an agent, he had always had therapy, but this time it was more personal than getting over some mission that had gone bad or even gone well. The emotions were raw and intense, but he owed it to Normalinda to continue their relationship with a clearer head and open heart. It would take time, but Normalinda was willing to walk out the process with Xavier. Love is truly stronger than death.

Normalinda left the law firm and started her own practice so that she would have the freedom to spend as much time with Xavier as possible. She needed a clean slate as well. There were too many memories at the firm, with Harold and Miller. She needed her own space, place, and to be able to run her practice like she wanted and serve the clients who meant the most to her.

Normalinda asked Xavier to accompany her to see her parents one weekend in Lexington. They pulled up in the curved drive way of her parents' home in Lexington, Kentucky. They had long moved from that little farm house on the Miller place. Normalinda made sure of that.

"You ready?"

"Ready as I'll ever be," he said.

They exited Xavier's newly purchased SUV and walked hand in hand up the six steps to the front door. Normalinda rang the doorbell and when the door opened, a young man opened the door and stood in the doorway looking from left to right at Normalinda then to Xavier. He was a younger, spitting image version of Xavier. He had the same eyes, hair, skin, mouth and body build as Xavier.

"Hey, Mom, who's he?"

"Mom?" Xavier looked at Normalinda with millions of questions.

"Hey, baby, I have somebody for you to meet. This is your father, Xavier Hernandez."

"My father?"

"My son?"

"Yes, your father and, yes, your son," she confirmed.

Xavier Carlton Martin stretched forth his hand and said, "Nice to meet you finally. Where have you been?"

Xavier Hernandez stretched his hand and grasped the young man's firmly. "Nice to meet you finally as well. As to your second question, I have been lost, running around the world handling business, but I never knew that you existed. Please know that I would have never ignored you if I had known you were mine. I spent years being ignored and denied by my own father. With that behind me, I want to make it up to you by getting to know you and, hopefully, build a home with you and your mom and finally have the family I've always dreamed of."

"Well, we'll have to figure that out as we go," young Xavier said to his father.

"My pleasure," Xavier Sr. said.

"Home is where the heart is, and I pray that your heart stays with us. It's time for you to get to know your son," Normalinda added with tears running down her face.

"Gladly, but you've got to be patient with me. I don't know how to be a father yet and I've never been a husband. It'll take time, so be patient with me."

"I'll be glad to show you how to be a father but it's left up to my mom if she wants a husband," the young boy said.

"Hush, both of you. The way it smells inside, it must be time to eat," Normalinda said.

"It is," Xavier Jr. moved aside and they stepped inside.

"Wow, you're the same height as I am," Xavier Sr. said.

Xavier Jr. said nothing but only smiled.

Six Months Later...

They were all assembled for Xavier and Normalinda's wedding. A small affair but beautiful and elegant. Xavier finally had the family that he always wanted, a gorgeous wife and a handsome son.

About the Author
Julia A. Royston/Kadance Royal

Julia Royston is an author, publisher, speaker and coach.

Kadance Royal is the official pen name of Julia Royston under the publishing imprint, Royal Media and Publishing established in 2015.

Julia and her husband, Brian, spend their time overseeing the operations of BK Royston Publishing, LLC, Royal Media Publishing, Book Business Bosses and BK Royston Foundation to provide quality, informative, inspirational and entertaining materials as well as writing and business consulting. By profession, Julia is a retired technology teacher/librarian.

To connect with Julia on all of her platforms, visit http://solo.to/juliaaroyston.

Men of Roberts Junction Series

The Men of Roberts Junction Series

Author
Kadance Royal

Another book by Julia A. Royston under the pen name of Kadance Royal is "Roberts Junction."

The first book written under this pen name.

Other Books by Julia A. Royston

Upcoming Series by Kadance Royal
Fall of 2022

Julia A. Royston/Kadance Royal Books!
Coming Fall 2022!

www.ingramcontent.com/pod-product-compliance
Lightning Source LLC
Chambersburg PA
CBHW050405030726
47503CB00006B/2026